200
cigarettes

ABOUT THE AUTHOR

Spencer Johns is a writer living in New York City.

200

cigarettes

a novel

Spencer Johns

based on the screenplay by Shana Larsen

Pocket Books

New York   London   Toronto   Sydney   Tokyo   Singapore

This book is a work of fiction. Names, characters, places and incidents are products of the author's imagination or are used fictitiously. Any resemblance to actual events or locales or persons, living or dead, is entirely coincidental.

An *Original* Publication of MTV Books / Pocket Books

POCKET BOOKS, a division of Simon & Schuster Inc.
1230 Avenue of the Americas, New York, NY 10020

ISBN: 0-671-03569-X

First MTV Books / Pocket Books trade paperback printing February 1999

10 9 8 7 6 5 4 3 2 1

Printed in the U.S.A.

QB/BP/✗

for J. A.

1

It's New Year's Eve 1981 and everybody in New York City wants to get laid. But this could also be said about the other 364 nights of the calendar. People are lonely all the time. But on December 31, you do feel the loneliness more. So you get drunk and you try to have sex. It's like birds flying south, salmon swimming north, dreamers going west—it's a force of nature you have to obey. Except it's not easy because the key to getting laid is to not think about getting laid. That's what makes New Year's Eve so difficult—everybody is forcing it, everybody's desperate, the clock is ticking, like you are taking an exam. It's a test of your attractiveness. And who wants to fail?

• • •

It's eight o'clock, Kevin and Lucy are in a taxi going down Second Avenue, New York City, New York. He's twenty-seven, she's twenty-six. He's tall, good-looking, a blond, just starting to lose his hair. She's a dyed blonde, a pretty girl with large sad eyes. She's medium height, a nice figure, but, in her mind, small breasts. She wishes often that her breasts were bigger. She'd feel more feminine.

Kevin and Lucy are platonic friends. They met five years ago when they were both new in the city and going out with other people. And since then they've never been single at the same time. They're both painters, but they make their living working *for* galleries. Answering phones, hanging the art.

Tonight, Kevin's wearing a black peacoat, black jeans, and a black turtleneck. Lucy's wearing black stockings, a black miniskirt, a black turtleneck, and a black leather jacket. They're both dressed so black they can hardly see each other's bodies in the black back seat of the cab.

Kevin is drunk; he already had five beers at his place before picking up Lucy. He's got a beer bottle in his hand that he's pretending to steer, like a little kid with one of those fake plastic steering wheels.

Lucy is putting on dark red lipstick, studying herself in her little compact mirror. She always feels stronger after she puts on her lipstick, like it's armor. *I'm going into battle. Somebody tonight will want to kiss this mouth.*

The cabbie, who has long, cool dreadlocks, is smoking a joint and blasting disco music out of his radio. He figures there's no reason why he shouldn't get to party on New Year's Eve. *I'm going to have a good time AND make money.*

He looks in the rearview mirror. The white boy is playing

2

with his beer bottle. He thinks of saying something—he doesn't want to smell stale beer all night—but he holds his tongue. He wants a good tip. He takes a hit off his joint. Stays cool. Traffic is thick. Everybody is out on New Year's Eve.

Kevin leans forward and shouts with his beer breath into the cabbie's ear, "Crank it . . . New Year's Eve . . . Crank it!" Kevin leans back, satisfied.

The cabbie tries to find Lucy's eyes in the rearview mirror. But she's looking at herself in her little mirror. He talks to her anyway. "Your friend okay back there?"

She doesn't look up. She wants to make her mouth a beautiful, perfect thing. "Sure. He's fine."

Kevin puts his steering-wheel bottle between his legs and unrolls his window. The fresh air feels good on his face, excites him. "Rock on!" he shouts to Second Avenue, to New York, to the world.

"What's he doing?" asks the cabbie. This kid is bumming him out. "He's not getting sick back there is he?"

"He has no life," shouts Lucy over the music, putting away her mirror. Her mouth is a sexy, red rose. Kevin keeps his head out. "His girlfriend left him last night. And that's just the tip of the fucking iceberg."

"Oh, yeah?" The cabbie likes to hear good stories. Makes the job interesting. Stories and the pot. He lowers the music a notch.

Kevin pulls his head back inside and rolls up the window. They're talking about him. He's going to tell this driver about his ex, cabbies are good for that, like bartenders and priests and shrinks. Good to vent at.

"She's a bitch," he shouts. "I have no life whatsoever. I'm a

3

loser." He looks at Lucy. He's going to make this group therapy, confront *her* now. "And you're dragging me to some stupid New Year's Eve party." Then he looks backs to the driver, his temporary shrink. "And as if all this wasn't depressing enough, it's my birthday."

"You didn't want to celebrate your birthday," says Lucy, hurt that maybe he's implying that she's not a good friend because she didn't get him a present. Kevin had told her, as always, not to even bring up his birthday.

Kevin ignores Lucy, and looks at the driver's mildly stoned eyes. "I ask you, how perfect is that? Dumped . . . Getting older . . . New Year's Eve."

"I offered to throw you a party," says Lucy, upset. Kevin's pulling his usual New Year's Eve-poor-me-birthday-bullshit, and she feels blamed. She doesn't like to be blamed.

"Trust me—I don't want a party," says Kevin. "I just want to *party.*"

"You do this every year, Kevin. You ruin a perfectly good holiday with your stupid birthday bullshit!"

"Hey, I'm sorry it's my birthday, okay? In fact, I'm sorry I was born at all! Are you happy now?"

The cabbie, like a good therapist, lets them duke it out.

"Fuck you," says Lucy.

"Fuck you," says Kevin.

"Pull over," says Lucy to the cabbie. He stops in front of a Korean deli on Eleventh Street and Second Avenue. "I'll be right back," she says to the cabbie, and then to Kevin, getting in the last word, "Fuck you, again." She slams the door.

Kevin lights a cigarette to calm his nerves.

"Sorry, but there's no smoking in my cab," says the driver.

4

"What are you talking about? You're smoking."

"I'm not smoking what you're smoking." The cabbie doesn't like the smell of beer or cigarettes in his car. Marijuana, on the other hand, smells beautiful.

Kevin throws his cigarette out the window. He looks into the cabbie's rear-view-mirror eyes. "Great. You know what? That's perfect." His own sarcasm tastes bitter in his mouth. His whole life sucks. He can't even smoke a cigarette. *But I should quit anyway. Have to do something right. Quit smoking. Tomorrow. A New Year's resolution.*

The cabbie takes a nice hit off his joint. He wants to help this birthday boy. "Man, you have got to relax," he says. "I mean, will you look around you? Everyone's having a good time. They're out there drinking, fighting, pissing on the street, loving the ladies." He turns to give the guy the full benefit of his wisdom, to make it personal, face to face. "Let me tell you something, my man. This is not the way to celebrate. The ladies are looking to drop a burden, not carry one. Don't be a burden, man . . . Want to know why I succeed?"

"No."

"First—very important—you have to smile. A lot." The cabbie smiles to demonstrate. "Second, don't talk about death. That'll stink up the whole party, turns women off. And third," the cabbie turns the disco up real loud, "you feel it?" he shouts. "You follow? Music, man, feel the music. Love is all about rhythm."

Kevin stares at the cabbie. He feels sick. *I'm a loser getting advice from a loser.* Lucy opens the cab door. She hands Kevin a large paper bag. She tells the cabbie to take them down to Fourth Street. The cabbie pulls into the traffic.

"What's this?" says Kevin, holding the paper bag, his beer bottle still between his legs, forgotten.

"Your present, fuckhead. Open it." Kevin's hopes spark for a second, for a moment he's touched. He opens the bag. It's a carton of Marlboros. Two hundred cigarettes. His resolution is already fucked. Like everything else.

"Happy birthday," says Lucy, wanting to be a little sweet after all.

It's eight-ten; Monica has just put a bowl of crab dip on her long dining-room table. She's throwing the party that Kevin and Lucy are coming to.

On the table, there are also chips, salsa, cheese, guacamole, bottles of white wine, vodka, rum, soda, and, underneath the table, a case of cheap champagne, with a few bottles chilling in the fridge along with all the six-packs of beer. Monica's hoping too that people will bring their own booze. She also hopes nobody vomits tonight. She knows that this is a somewhat unreasonable hope.

She wants the party to be a success and she has one other little wish for the night—that one of the guests, preferably a real stud, an unexpected, successful stranger, will be spending the night. So she's all decked out in her best black cocktail dress, which accentuates her full bosom. And she went to the salon, so her auburn hair after its washing and trim has a nice bounce. She glances at the long mirror on the wall to check herself out. *Oh, God, my ass looks big. Why is my ass always big? This year I'm going to stick with a diet.*

She turns away from the mirror quickly, so as to stop torturing herself. She's twenty-seven and she's been a little plump ever since she put on those fifteen pounds that first semester freshman year. *I never should have gone to college.* To get her mind off of fat-thoughts, she surveys her apartment, to see if there's anything that needs to be done for the party. It's all set. Her friend Hillary, who never has to diet, sits on one of the chairs against the wall. Hillary and Monica used to work together at *Elle.* Now Hillary is at *Allure.*

Hillary is bored, smoking. Lost in her own world. Her long legs are sloppily crossed. She too is wearing a black cocktail dress that's the color of her jet-black hair. She has an attractive, perpetually bored face—a long nose, high cheekbones, an arrogant mouth. *I hope somebody brings some coke.* She stares at the blinking lights of Monica's Christmas tree.

Monica's proud of her tree. Her large Great Jones Street loft has a nice Christmassy feeling because of the tree, and she has hung green and red banners on the wall that say "Happy New Year!" And there are festive balloons kissing the ceiling. She has pushed all her furniture off to the sides; her bedroom in the far corner will be the coatroom, but off-limits. She'll let her apartment be trashed for the party, but not her bedroom. Not where she and Mr. Perfect Unexpected Hero will be ushering in the New Year. And above her bed, where all this bliss will take place, is the poster of her all-time love object, her favorite musician and personal god—Elvis Costello.

She turns back to the table and takes a taste of the dip. It's not bad, but suddenly she's overwhelmed, as if with a religious epiphany, by the stupidity and folly of the whole enterprise. Only an insane person throws a New Year's Eve party! Only an insane person spends an hour making *crab dip!*

"What was I thinking?" she asks the uninterested Hillary. "Do you realize I got this recipe off a box of cream cheese? I don't even recognize myself anymore. I hate parties. I hate giving them and I hate going to them. But at least when I'm going to them I'm not responsible for how horrible they are— and this one's going to be the worst. I can feel it. Nobody's coming. *No,* the losers will be here. All the people I hate will be here. All my old boyfriends and their new more attractive girlfriends will be here. Throwing a New Year's party is like an invitation for abuse. It's like the last desperate act of someone who hasn't had a lasting relationship since junior high."

"You dated in junior high?" asks Hillary, vaguely impressed that Monica might have been sexually active in the eighth grade, though not too concerned that her friend seems to be losing it.

"Why am I doing this?" asks Monica, not so much to Hillary as to herself. "Why am I subjecting myself to this? I think I'm going to be sick." She runs for the toilet.

3

Kevin and Lucy enter Jack Dempsey's, an Irish bar on Second Avenue, between Third and Fourth Streets. It is one crosstown block from Monica's party.

Jack Dempsey's is a big place with a bar in front and a back room filled with tables and a pool table. Drunken Kevin leads the way in and Lucy trails behind him. He's bumping into people as he makes his way through the crowd near the bar. He doesn't like crowds, especially tonight. He's bumping into people, on purpose, trying to provoke them. *Fuck you. Fuck you. Fuck you.*

He knocks into a young woman drinking a beer. She thinks it's her fault, that she must have stepped into him. "Sorry," she says.

"Yeah. Right," says Kevin. Then he gives a good hockey

check to a big Irishman, who spills his beer. The big guy glares at Kevin.

"What, you want a piece of me?" Kevin snaps.

Lucy pulls him away, smiles at the Irishman. "I'm sorry, I'm sorry," she says. The big guy lets it go; it's too early to start fighting. Lucy grabs a table. They sit down. Kevin's scowling.

"You're such an asshole, don't bump into people like that," she says, and then she notices something. "Hey, where's the carton of cigs I got you?"

Kevin's scowl turns into a look of contrition and remorse. "Oh, my God," he says, "I put them on the floor when I paid that stoned cabbie. I'm really sorry."

"You really are an asshole. That's how you treat my birthday present to you? I need a drink . . . And I'll get one for you too, another birthday present. Try not to spill it."

Lucy heads for the bar. Kevin calls after: "I'm sorry about the cigarettes. It was a mistake." But Lucy doesn't acknowledge his apology, and Kevin has gone from being aggressive to depressive, and he hangs his head and runs his fingers through his thinning blond hair. His woes increase. *I have no life. I'm going bald.*

• • •

Two tables away from the mildly balding Kevin, Bridget sits with Eric, who has a full head of hair. These two are also going to Monica's party. Bridget is a cute redhead with big blue eyes and freckles on her nose. She's twenty-four and a photographer—she primarily does artistic self-portraits. To support herself she works as a receptionist for an advertising agency.

Eric is a handsome, intense-looking twenty-eight-year-old

painter with a trust fund, dark curly hair, and a slightly bent nose. He has just told Bridget that he used to go out with Monica, the host of the party he's taking her to. This is horrifying to Bridget. She and Eric have been going out for a month.

"You used to go out with her?" she asks, to make sure she heard him correctly.

"It was a long time ago."

"I don't believe this! I don't believe you're dragging me to one of your old girlfriends' parties on New Year's Eve!"

"I told you, it was a long time ago."

"Oh, yeah? How long ago?"

"I don't know. We broke up maybe six months ago." Eric fingers his pack of Marlboros. This conversation is making him want to smoke, but he doesn't have matches.

"Six months? You think that's a long time?"

"Yeah, I do. I think six months is a considerable length of time."

This discussion of relationship timetables is interrupted by Caitlyn, Bridget's friend from their days in art school at Cooper Union. She arrives at their table with three beers. Eric invited Bridget to the party and Bridget invited Caitlyn, who is a tiny, voluptuous brunette. She's wearing a lot of eye makeup and a deep dark red lipstick. She's also got on her tightest sweater and her tightest jeans. She really wants to meet somebody tonight. She put her diaphragm in her purse an hour ago with conviction.

She doesn't like this bar because it doesn't seem to have any good-looking single men. The guy with the thin blond hair two tables over isn't bad, but he looks tormented and he seems to be waiting for somebody. But if all else fails, Caitlyn has a secret plan to get laid, if not tonight, then very soon.

She puts down the three beers, takes her seat, and says with disgust to Bridget and Eric, "Can you believe this place?"

Bridget ignores this and asks Caitlyn, "Do you think six months is a long time to have been broken up with somebody?"

"I guess—if it's a clean break," she says, then she slides a matchbook over to Eric, the one he asked her to get at the bar, the one she has prepared in a special way. "Here are the matches you wanted."

"Thanks." He lights up.

Bridget doesn't want them to get off the subject, so she addresses Caitlyn: "He just told me he used to go out with the bitch who's throwing this party tonight."

To Caitlyn this violates all rules of dating and parties and fucking. "You went out with the host?"

Both she and Bridget stare at Eric. He doesn't like the way they're looking at him. He's broken some kind of female rule of etiquette. He always screws up with women. He tries to explain. "I only said we'd go because she's afraid no one's going to show up."

"You *spoke* to her?" Bridget asks, horrified, knee-jerk jealous.

"Yeah, when she invited me."

Caitlyn doesn't like the sound of this party—will it be dead? She thinks of her diaphragm in her purse. "You think your ex is right? About no one showing up?"

Before he can answer, Bridget announces, "Well, I'm not going." Then she stands up and says to Caitlyn, "Let's go to the bathroom."

• • •

Lucy and Kevin are having their drinks, rum and Cokes. Kevin is looking mildly suicidal; he's still fingering his thin hair.

Lucy wants to cheer him up; she's forgiven him for losing the cigarettes. She also wants to salvage the night before it's too late. "Isn't this great?" she says. "See how much fun we're having."

Kevin responds by pantomiming a vomit into his glass. False cheeriness doesn't work, so she tries a new tactic, something to jolt Kevin out of his self-centered torment—some homophobic teasing. "I think the bartender likes you."

"He doesn't like me. He likes you."

"You think so?" she asks. Kevin is only joking back at her, but she's desperate for something life-affirming, so she turns and looks at the bartender. He happens to glance up at that precise moment and he smiles at her, and he's got a great smile. He doesn't look like the brightest guy in the world, but that's because he's off-balance in the looks department—he's gorgeous. The kind of guy that played quarterback in high school. The kind of guy who tries to model or go to Hollywood. The kind of guy who does a lot of bartending.

"He is so cute. Isn't he?" she asks Kevin.

"Adorable," he says, and then he actually does look at the bartender. He envies the guy his full head of quarterback hair. He calls to the barkeep. "Hey, you're a fox!" The bartender doesn't hear him.

Lucy is still checking him out. "You think I should invite him to this party? He's got to be depressed, working on New Year's Eve."

"Everyone's depressed on New Year's Eve," says Kevin.

"No one's depressed but you." She finishes off her rum and Coke. "See? I'm having a wonderful time."

"You're not having a wonderful time," he says. "No one is. Look around. There's this ridiculous obligation on New Year's Eve to enjoy yourself, but no matter what, you never match your own unrealistic expectations of what you should be doing. Every year it's the same desperate scrambling to surround yourself with as many people as possible—to get to some stupid party, so you can stand around pretending to be happy all night when really your girlfriend left you and you have no career."

Lucy's not sure how much more of Kevin she can take. "Are you going to be like this all night?"

Kevin ponders this question a moment. He really would like to think that he won't be depressing company all night. So he tries to rally himself inside himself, to think of some reason to enjoy being alive. He roots around in his mind, but it's like an empty wallet, it's like a dresser drawer with no clean clothes. Nothing comes to him. He looks at his friend and says miserably, but honestly, "I'm going to be like this all night."

4

Monica is out of the bathroom. She didn't get sick, but it was better to be safe than sorry. She can't believe she almost threw up *before* her party. That would have been a bad omen, especially since she wants to have a classy, vomit-free celebration.

So she and Hillary are just sitting there, waiting, and drinking white wine out of clear plastic glasses. They sit in chairs against the walls on opposite sides of the loft.

"What time is it?" Monica asks.

Hillary lifts her arm as if it weighs a great deal. "Almost eight-thirty."

They each take sips of their wine. Hillary yawns a yawn of profound weariness and boredom. Monica glares at her. *Why can't that bitch be supportive? She's making me feel worse. I'm doomed, this party is doomed. If no one shows up I'll kill myself . . . Then they'll all feel guilty and have to come to my funeral. I'll be popular when I'm dead.*

5

It's eight-thirty and Val and Stephie are walking east on Third Street. Val is Monica's cousin. She's been invited to the party and she's brought along Stephie, her best friend. They're both juniors at Ronkonkoma High School in Long Island, and they're both wearing winter jean jackets with fringes and high-heeled boots. They have glitter eye-makeup on and a lot of rouge. They're both Italian and dark-haired. Val is sexy; she has a wild, curious-about-life look to her, and she has pretty green eyes. Stephie is less attractive. She's a little plain, even with the eye glitter. And her mouth has a nervous look to it. She's more apt to frown than smile. She looks like she'll be a Long Island housewife in ten years, drinking coffee over the sink and worrying about bills. But right now she's sixteen and excited to be in New York. Scared too, but also excited.

Val is walking faster than Stephie, she's the leader. She turned seventeen a week ago; Val is still a sweet sixteen.

They've been walking east for about ten minutes. They took the subway to West Fourth Street, having first arrived in New York at Penn Station.

"Just promise me we won't go past Avenue A," says Stephie.

"How many times I got to tell you we're not going there?"

They both speak with harsh Long Island accents, which makes everything sound mildly like an argument or a negotiation at a yard sale.

"I'm serious, I know a girl who got raped on B," says Stephie, who, as well she should, has a great fear of rape. Her mother is always talking about rape and how Stephie has to avoid it. And Stephie thinks it would be especially bad to be raped because she's still a virgin, and she wants to lose her virginity to someone special. What if she lost it to a rapist?

"Okay, okay," says Val, wanting to placate her friend. "We're not going on Avenue B, okay?"

Stephie feels reassured. "It's so cool we're hanging out with a band on New Year's Eve," she says. Stephie loves bands. She especially loves Bruce Springsteen, even though she's from Long Island and not from New Jersey. But she'd like to be from New Jersey so she could have that in common with Bruce. When she imagines losing her virginity, she wishes she could lose it to him, the Boss. "So when are we going to meet these band guys?"

"I told you, after the party."

"So what about this party? Are there gonna be guys there? Your cousin know any guys?"

"Yeah, she knows guys, but they're mostly weird like her."

19

"I like weird guys. I mean, I can get into that shit. Where's this party anyway, SoHo?" Stephie's trying to act hip, cool.

"NoHo."

"I thought you said SoHo."

"No, I said NoHo."

"NoHo? What kind of place is NoHo? Sounds bad, like No Where or something."

"Sorreee," says Val. "But whatever it is, it's just up ahead . . . Wait a minute." Val stops in front of an old condemned building at 21 East Third Street. There are posters on the building of a woman in a wedding gown wielding an ax to the bust of Sigmund Freud.

"What's the matter?" asks Stephie. She knows right away that something is wrong.

"I thought this was the place," says Val.

Stephie looks at the building, with its plywood for windows, its weird posters of a bride with an ax attacking the sculpture of some old man's head. "This shithole?"

Val removes a crumpled piece of paper from her jean-jacket pocket. "Yeah. This is the address she gave me."

"You're shitting me."

Val studies the paper. "I don't believe it. I mean, this is the address I wrote down." What Val doesn't realize is that her cousin told her 21 Great Jones Street, not 21 East Third Street. But Val didn't write down the Great Jones part, she didn't think she'd need to, because her cousin told her that Great Jones is the same thing as East Third Street. And it is the same street, essentially—for two blocks between Broadway and Bowery— but it has its own numbers, separate from Third Street. So there's a 21 Great Jones and a 21 East Third. Two different places. Val and Stephie are on the wrong side of Bowery, only half a block from Monica's, but they don't know it.

"Call your cousin up," says Stephie.

"I don't have her number. She called me, invited me. She was afraid nobody would come to her party."

"You don't have her number? What the fuck you carrying in that purse, a fucking Encyclopedia Britannica?" Stephie, even though she's a nice girl and has never fucked, employs the word "fuck" and all its grammatical variations with great frequency. But this isn't an indication of poor character. In Ronkonkoma, and in most of America, the word is quite divorced from its actual meaning. It's simply a common curse, just a little bit worse than "shit" or "damn."

"I don't know what I have in my purse," says Val. "I got makeup and stuff in there."

Stephie has a low threshold for panicking in crisis situations, and she's especially overwhelmed by being in New York City for the first time without her parents. "Makeup and stuff?" she says. "We're fucked! We're totally fucked on New Year's Eve with a purse full of makeup and this shithole building address!"

Val, who is always their leader, is momentarily at a loss. "What should we do?"

"There's nothing we can do! We're fucked." *I'm going to be raped on New Year's Eve, I know it.*

"I'll call and see if she's listed. You got a dime?"

Stephie gives her a dime. She feels like it's the most important dime she's ever had.

21

6

Eric is alone at the table. Bridget and Caitlyn are still in the bathroom. He looks around, bored. The blond guy two tables over looks familiar. But Eric can't place him. *Probably know him from the art world.* Eric takes out another cigarette and opens up the matchbook Caitlyn gave him, and inside she's written her name and phone number. *Holy shit. This is fucked up.* He stays calm and lights his cigarette and puts the matches in his shirt pocket. He's got to make sure to keep these matches away from Bridget. He's flustered by the whole thing, but also flattered—Caitlyn must really want him.

Bridget and Caitlyn are in the bathroom, standing in front of the mirror. Bridget is leaning against the sink, smoking, and Caitlyn is fixing her lipstick.

Bridget exhales a thin gray cloud of smoke and says, "Do

you think I'm overreacting about this old girlfriend thing?"

"Absolutely not," says Caitlyn, thinking about the match-book. This is her window of opportunity.

"I mean, they only broke up about six months ago, right?"

"Please, they're practically still going out," says Caitlyn, and it's all working out better than she hoped. If Bridget breaks up with Eric, then she's not stealing him away. She's on steady, moral ground.

Bridget has made up her mind. It's over with Eric. "It's too bad in a way," she says. "He was kind of . . . nice, you know."

"He was too nice. You need somebody with some edge. Some life to him, you know, a little bit of danger to his person-ality." She finishes with her lipstick. Her mouth looks good. She feels good.

"Yeah—and then today he takes me by his gallery, to see his new show? And it sucks."

This shocks Caitlyn. Like Bridget, she too is a struggling artist, specializing in self-referential sculptures and installa-tions, and one of the things that makes her covet Eric is that he's the only *successful* artist she knows. The only one who actually has shows at galleries. *And* he has a trust fund. "His paintings suck?"

"I'm telling you, you wouldn't believe his work. It's like all big abstract vaginas or something."

"Oh, God. I hate abstract." But she stops a second and thinks the guy can't be too bad—he has shows, after all. What other painters actually have shows? She has to defend her man. Her soon-to-be-man, that is. "But at least he has a gallery; I mean, that's something."

Bridget puts her cigarette out in the sink. "So what? He's also really bad in bed."

Caitlyn feels like she's been punched. "He's bad in bed?"

"The worst."

Caitlyn feels sick. The *matchbook*. She needs a cigarette to calm her nerves. To hell with her fresh lipstick. "Can I have a cigarette?" she asks. Bridget gives her one and the two friends stay in the bathroom and smoke.

● ● ●

Lucy is standing at the bar, writing the address of Monica's party on a napkin. She and Kevin have moved their drinking to the bar so that Lucy can flirt with the bartender, and it's already working. The bartender is smiling at Lucy while she writes on the napkin. He thinks it's sweet that this blonde with these big eyes is inviting him to a New Year's party. He actually gets off at ten—he's been on since noon—so he figures he'll check this party out.

Kevin is standing behind Lucy. He is a zombie, filled with depression and booze. Lucy finishes writing on the napkin and slides it to the handsome quarterback-bartender.

"So if you want to check it out," Lucy says, "when you get off work . . ."

"Yeah, thanks a lot," he says.

"It's going to be a great party. Lots of people . . . and me, of course. I'll be there, too, you know, with him." She nods off-handedly toward Kevin.

The bartender puts the napkin in his pocket. "Great. Well, thanks a lot." He moves to the other end of the bar, where the big Irishman needs a refill.

Lucy suddenly realizes she may have fucked up. *Shit.* She calls after him, "Wait, I don't mean *with* him! Because we're not together! We're just friends."

But the bartender can't hear her, the place is noisy and he's got plenty of business at the other end.

"Shit. He is so cute. You think he heard me?"

Kevin doesn't answer her question. He's in his own self-centered drunken world. He launches into a monologue as if he and Lucy had been having a conversation about his break-up: "I mean, it's inevitable, you know? You let someone move in with you, you make all these little compromises to smooth things along—and before you know it, your entire life is changed. Suddenly you're on a macrobiotic diet and listening to Joni Mitchell. And you know what happens then? One day they turn to you and they say, 'You've changed. You're not the same person I fell in love with.' And they dump you."

"What do you expect?" asks Lucy. "You always choose these angry, condescending, and emasculating women. You should find someone who likes you the way you are."

"Yeah. And why would anyone possibly like me the way I am?"

Lucy contemplates this a moment, then says, "I have no idea . . . Just finish your drink so I can get that bartender back over here."

7

Val is at a pay phone at the corner of Third Street and First Avenue. She holds the cold receiver to her ear. Stephie is standing next to her, and she's freezing and worried. She smokes a cigarette. Val hangs up.

"So?" asks Stephie.

"She ain't listed."

"We're gonna end up on B, I know it."

"We're not gonna end up on B, okay?" Val is pissed at Stephie. *What a fucking whiner, I should have left her back in Ronkonkoma.*

"So where the fuck are we gonna go?"

"I don't know."

"What about this band you been talking about? Can't we just meet them now and skip the party?"

"No, it's too early."

"Well, I'm freezing my ass off, here."

"You should have worn a sweater."

"Where the fuck are we gonna go? We don't know anybody."

"Maybe we'll meet somebody."

"What?" Stephie can't believe this. Meet strangers in New York? *Val's gone off the deep end, she's gonna get us killed.*

"You know," says Val. "Maybe we'll meet some people."

"What are you, on another planet? You don't meet people on the street. Even at a party you don't meet people. You just stand there talking to people you know already."

"Let's just keep walking." Val crosses First Avenue and Stephie follows. "It's got to be around here somewhere," says Val. "I'll know the place when I see it. I been there once."

On the other side of First Avenue, Stephie stops walking. "Call your mother."

Val stops and turns to Stephie. "My mother?"

"Yeah, she's got your cousin's number, don't she?"

"I can't call her. She thinks I'm at your house tonight."

Val starts walking again. Stephie grabs her arm. "Val, listen to me. We are in deep shit here. I say we either call your mother for the number or get the train back to Ronkonkoma."

Val pulls her arm away from Stephie and keeps walking east, even though she has no idea where she's going.

Stephie doesn't move. She watches Val march off. She wonders if she should go back to the train station by herself. *Val will think I'm so uncool.* She runs after Val and calls out, "You just stay the fuck away from B!"

27

8

Two more people are on their way to Monica's party—Jack and Cindy. It's their first *official* date. They met each other the night before at a bar, and though their encounter was quite intimate, a pickup doesn't count as an official date.

Jack is twenty-seven and an actor. He does catering on the side to pay the bills when things are slow. He has all-American good looks—broad shoulders, sandy blond hair, clear skin, and kind blue eyes.

Cindy is adorable, with chestnut brown hair and a face with cherry-red cheeks that make her look sixteen even though she's twenty-four. She works at *The New Yorker* as a fact-checker and all-around gofer. Her hair is piled up—she's aspiring for an Audrey Hepburn look—but it doesn't appear like it will hold. The cold December winds are starting to have their way with her coiffure.

They're walking down Second Avenue and they come to Jack Dempsey's, everybody's favorite East Village Irish bar. "You want to stop for a drink?" asks Jack.

"I don't know. Do you?"

Jack looks at his watch. "It's still early. I hate getting to a party before everyone else."

"Oh, okay. We could get a drink, I mean, if you want to."

"Well, I don't want to force you to drink against your will. Do you want to stop for a drink?"

"Sure. If you do." Her ambivalence annoys Jack, and she senses this. "Look, Jack, we don't have to do this," she says.

"It's just a drink," he says. He doesn't understand why she's making a federal case out of going into Jack Dempsey's.

"No, I mean about going to the party."

"You don't want to go to the party?"

"I just mean it's New Year's Eve and you don't have to spend it with me just because of, you know . . . what happened last night. We don't know each other very well and . . ." Her voice trails off.

Jack looks at Cindy. He wants to fix this situation. It's not a big deal. He takes a breath. "I know it's our first date and everything, and it's weird to have a first date on New Year's. But we had a nice time last night and so we can have a nice time tonight. We just have to relax and enjoy each other's company."

Cindy feels relieved. *Maybe he is sweet. Maybe he does want to be with me.* "Okay," she says.

"So, just to be clear—you do want to get a drink and then go to the party?"

"Well . . . sure. I mean, if you do."

This indecisiveness is annoying to Jack, but he takes another deep breath. He's got to be in charge of everything with this girl. "Okay, let's get a drink then," he says, falsely cheery, though Cindy doesn't detect this, and he opens the door to Jack Dempsey's for her. She walks in, happy to be going for a drink. Happy to be with Jack. He, on the other hand, is going through the motions. He's not finding Cindy to be much fun—she's too nervous and wishy-washy—and he wonders if he might have been better off going solo this New Year's Eve and seeing if he got lucky. But it's too late for that now, so he does hope a few drinks might relax her a little.

9

Monica is lying on the floor of her loft, staring at the balloons on the ceiling. She wonders if she popped a balloon and put it over her head if she would suffocate. That could be a good way to kill herself. Symbolic too. Death by New Year's Eve balloon.

Hillary walks over to the buffet table, lifts the crab dip, sniffs it, and puts it back down. She pours herself another cup of wine.

"Nobody's coming," says Monica, as if from her grave. "This is it. I have no friends and everybody hates me."

"It's only nine o'clock," says Hillary.

"What are they all doing? Just walking the streets out there? Just walking the streets like zombies because it's too uncool to be prompt?"

"I'm worried about you," says Hillary, attempting compassion. "I think you might be heading for a breakdown." She sips her wine. Her thoughts go back to herself, her love life. "You think there's going to be any interesting guys here tonight?"

"Interesting guys?"

"Yeah, because I think I'm finally over Lenny. I think I'm ready to start dating again."

Monica stands up. "Well, congratulations, Hillary. Over Lenny. I'm happy to hear about it." She heads for the table, for another glass of wine.

"After all," says Hillary, "what better night to start over than New Year's Eve? That is, unless you're right and no one shows up."

"Well, if they do, you have my word: Any interesting guy walks through the door, he's yours."

"Really?"

"You can have first pick. I'll usher them right over to you."

"But not in an obvious way. I don't want to look desperate."

"Desperate? You could stand there naked with a mattress strapped to your back and still look like you were playing hard to get."

"You think that could work? A mattress on the back . . . But you sure you don't mind giving me first pick? Because I know it's been a while since you've had any . . . you know, dates."

"Hillary, I promise you—I honestly could not give a shit about anything right now except this incredibly humiliating party-giving experience. I just wish it was over and I'd had a good time."

Monica has lowered her expectations for the night. She doesn't care if she meets Mr. Unexpected Hero. She just wants a Mr. or Ms. Expected Guest. Anybody, even her little cousin Val from Ronkonkoma.

10

Lucy, trying to have as much face time with the bartender as possible, has quickly ordered and then downed four rum and Cokes, and now has her head down on the bar. Being something of a lightweight, she has caught up to Kevin in drunkenness.

Kevin, meanwhile, is talking to the man next to him, a forty-year-old bald tax adjuster who just wants to drink in silence. Kevin, of course, is oblivious to this and is pouring out all his woes to the man.

"And then this idiot—this glorified file clerk—has the nerve to tell me my work is too cerebral. I thought at first he said 'too cereal.' I mean, what does he want? Paintings of flowers or a barn? Maybe a still life of some apples. Or tomato cans. They either want an Andy Warhol or an Edward Hopper. Why not a Kevin Gerber? It's sick. And this moron is a curator at a gallery! Where the hell do they get these people?"

Lucy, agitated by the annoying sounds of Kevin's complaining, moans quite loudly. She opens an eye and sees that the bar is spinning. At the center of the spinning is the object of her desire—the bartender. Then a nose with blond nostril hairs blocks her vision. It's Kevin's nose.

"Lucy? Are you all right?"

She doesn't lift her head off the bar. "Oh, God. I can't believe how drunk I am."

"You're certainly hiding it well."

"You're right about New Year's Eve. It sucks. That bartender doesn't even know I'm alive. He's even stopped the refills on our peanut bowl." She calls to the quarterback. "Hey, can I get some peanuts over here?"

"Maybe lift your head up. You're slurring your words . . . Did you tell him to bring his penis over here?" asks Kevin.

"No, peanuts."

"Well, it sounded like penis. An obvious Freudian slip."

"I said peanuts, you idiot." And then Lucy, still having not captured the bartender's attention, lifts her drunken head off the bar and yells, "Peanuts! I need peanuts!"

And all along the bar people turn their head and stare at Lucy. They're sure they heard her shouting, "Penis! I need penis!"

• • •

Eric is still by himself. He smokes and drinks. He drinks Caitlyn's and Bridget's drinks. They've been in the bathroom forever.

Caitlyn and Bridget are still leaning on the counter by the sink, smoking more cigarettes. They listen to a girl fart, then pee. For a bathroom, it doesn't smell too bad, but also their smoking helps with that. Caitlyn's feeling like it's time to get this over with.

"Look," she says to Bridget. "You're just going to have to go out there and break up with this guy."

"I know. I should just get it over with."

The girl who was farting and peeing stands between the two and washes her hands.

"One clean break and we're out of here," says Caitlyn. The girl dries her hands with a paper towel and leaves.

"I just feel bad, you know?" says Bridget. "I mean, it's New Year's Eve . . . if I dump him now, I won't have a date."

"Oh, please, it's only nine," says Caitlyn. "We have three hours to find dates. We've had entire relationships that didn't last that long."

"You think there's going to be any guys at that party?"

"God, I hope so."

Caitlyn and Bridget both look in the mirror. Caitlyn smooths down her tight sweater. *My boobs look good tonight.*

Bridget puts a little powder on her nose freckles, but doesn't overdo it. *A lot of guys like freckles.*

• • •

Just outside the bathroom is the pool table. Jack is racking up the balls so that he and Cindy can play. She nervously sips from a glass of wine. Her winter coat is hanging on a peg, and she looks out of place in Jack Dempsey's—she's wearing a lovely and expensive white cocktail dress. It's like a short wedding gown. Jack finishes racking up the balls.

"Jack, I'm really bad at this," she says.

"Really? I figured you for a hardened professional." He smiles his good-looking smile, hoping to relax her. But she's not relaxed. He holds out the pool cue. "You want to break?" She stares at the cue like it's a gun. A loaded gun. "Look, it's just a game, right?" he asks.

"Right, just a game," she says and she takes the cue-rifle.

She puts her wine down on the rim of the pool table, to her right. She lines up behind the cue ball. She strikes it, but her follow-through is awkward, the stick is sliding out of her hand. Jack begins to say, "Watch your drink—" But it's too late. The end of the stick swings to the right, knocking her wineglass onto the pool table. The wine immediately stains the green felt. Cindy groans with embarrassment and spasmodically throws her hands into the air, as if to gesture, "Oh, no," but she's still holding the pool cue, which smashes into the cheap chandelier over the table. It makes a great glass-shattering sound and crashes to the green felt and onto the pool balls. Even over the din of the bar—the talking, the jukebox playing—the crash is like a loud firecracker and everyone turns and looks at Cindy. She holds the pool cue out from her like it's a smoking gun and she's guilty of murder and she wails, "Oh, God!"

Jack rushes to her and disarms her of the pool cue before things get worse, and Cindy, without her weapon, runs into the bathroom to hide.

11

Val and Stephie come to an avenue. Stephie innocently looks up at the street sign. It says: AVE. B. Val, unaware of the sign, waits for the light before she crosses the street. Stephie feels stuck, unable to move, like in a nightmare. She wants to cry out for help, but the words can't get out of her mouth. Then finally her tongue is loosened.

"Oh my God. Oh my God. We're on B. B!" Val has started to cross. Stephie calls after her friend. "Val! Val! This is it. This is B!"

Val keeps walking. Stephie's heart is gripped with terror. "Val," she pleads. "You've crossed B." B, which had always been an innocuous letter in the alphabet for Stephie, the second letter of twenty-six, which stood for nice things like

Bread and Bee and Ball and Bear and Bye-bye, now means Death and Rape and Satan and Torture.

Val looks back at the deranged Stephie. "Come on, we're almost there," she says, though they are farther away than ever from the party.

"No way! No way I'm taking one more step," she screams across the twenty-yard strip of asphalt that is Avenue B.

"What's the matter with you?" Val asks, wishing that she had a cooler friend. Couldn't Stephie live it up just once and not be scared? Val comes back across B to Stephie, to straighten her out. "Come on," she says, grabbing Stephie's arm. "Let's go."

"I'm not crossing B! I'm not moving."

"So freeze your fucking ass off. I'm going to the party."

"Val, I'm telling you, something terrible's gonna happen if we cross this street. I feel it in my gut."

"Will you get a hold of yourself? Nothing terrible's happening—we're just going to a party is all."

"You said the party was in SoHo!"

"I said NoHo."

"Well, NoHo ain't no fucking Avenue B! No way!"

Val glances around her, taking things in closely for the first time in a while. The tenement buildings are dark and their facades are stained with pollution and car exhaust. There's a bodega on the corner, emitting some yellowish light, but overall it's a dark and creepy and dangerous neighborhood.

"Val," whines Stephie, "please . . . will you please just call your mother?"

Some of Stephie's fear is getting under Val's skin. *Maybe we are going to be raped. But I'll just kick the guy in the balls and run.* "Okay, I'll call my mom," she says to Stephie and then she crosses B. She's not going to be a total wimp.

"Hey, where are you going?" cries Stephie. She had thought this madness was coming to an end.

"I gotta find a phone, don't I?"

"Yeah, but . . . you know there must be phones on A! A is better than B!"

Val turns and shoots Stephie the finger and then keeps walking, turning left up B. Stephie is still stuck on the corner. A force field of fear keeps her from setting foot on the road, as if B is a fast-moving river, and she is unable to swim.

But just then four male punk rockers with identical hairdos—spikes that look like ice picks dipped in blood— approach her. She feels that she has no choice, so, like Paul Newman and Robert Redford in *Butch Cassidy and the Sundance Kid,* she jumps into the River B, chasing after Val. *Oh, my God, I've crossed B. I'm not going to be a virgin anymore.*

Then, as she hurries up Avenue B, two men come out of a doorway and seem to follow her. She glances back at them. It's dark, the streetlights have mostly been busted, but she can see that they're in black leather jackets.

"We are so incredibly fucked," she says, out loud to herself. And then she catches up to Val at the corner of Fourth Street, her friend who is hell-bent on getting them killed and raped, and raped and killed.

12

Cindy is in the bathroom, splashing water on her face, trying to calm herself down after the humiliating debacle with the pool cue. Bridget and Caitlyn are watching her. They heard the crash through the bathroom door.

"What happened out there?" asks Bridget.

Cindy, seeking solace in the comfort of strangers, tells Bridget and Caitlyn what she has just done, that she was the cause of that startling noise. "I just . . . I can't believe I did that. I'm so stupid," she says.

"It doesn't sound so bad to me," says Bridget. "I bet it happens all the time. Sounds like that chandelier was hanging too low."

"Yeah," says Caitlyn. "This place is a dive anyway."

"You know," says Cindy, needing to open up more, "I don't

41

even know this guy I'm with. I only met him last night . . . He's an actor. I don't know, at first I thought, he seemed so nice that I thought maybe things would be okay, you know? But now everything I say and do comes out stupid! He makes me nervous. This is turning out to be the worst date of my entire life."

Bridget and Caitlyn look at one another. They don't have enough patience to hear someone they *know* go on like this, let alone a stranger. Cindy looks at them for sympathy, but senses their remove. "I'm sorry," she says. "I don't even know why I'm telling you this."

Bridget and Caitlyn head for the door. "Yeah, well . . . good luck," says Caitlyn.

"Yeah. Happy New Year," says Bridget.

They get outside the bathroom and Caitlyn says, "Do you believe that girl?"

"Really, get a shrink," says Bridget.

"Nice outfit, though."

"Yeah, for a wedding."

They walk over to Eric, while Cindy stares at herself in the bathroom mirror. Her makeup is smeared by the water she splashed herself with. She's forlorn, but not completely defeated. Out comes the lipstick, every woman's first line of defense. She begins to apply the phallic red stick to her mouth, but since everything is going wrong for Cindy, her applicator snaps against her sweet mouth and falls out of the tube. It caroms off the front of her cocktail dress, leaving a scarlet stripe on her breast, and then continues its tragic journey down into the bathroom sink. The sink is clogged and has a small pool of brownish water. In the water are the several cigarettes left behind by the plotting Bridget and Caitlyn.

Cindy is not quite rational. She needs her lipstick. She needs to fix her mouth. She figures she can rinse off her lipstick and put it back in the tube. She plunges her hand into the murky water to find it. She gets the thing, rinses it, and then puts it back in the tube. She raises the still germ-laden instrument to her mouth. It looms like a horrible red mini-penis. Before she applies it to her lips, she regains her sanity and throws the whole tube into the sink. To hell with fixing her mouth. She leaves the bathroom.

• • •

Bridget and Caitlyn rejoin the exasperated Eric. They were in the bathroom for almost twenty minutes.

"What the hell were you two doing back there?"

"Nothing," says Bridget.

"Nothing?"

Caitlyn waves an unlit cigarette in Eric's face. "You have a light for a girl?"

Eric lifts up the fat candleholder on the table toward Caitlyn's cigarette and says to Bridget, "You were gone at least twenty minutes!"

"I mean a match," says Caitlyn, pushing the candleholder back to the table.

"Eric, just relax," says Bridget.

"A match," says Caitlyn.

Eric reaches into his pocket and without thinking about it hands Caitlyn the matchbook with her phone number written inside.

"I've been sitting here all this time," says Eric. "I'm entitled to an explanation."

Caitlyn is relieved to have the matchbook back in her possession. "Thanks," she says, quite sincerely. *I can't believe I gave him my number and he's bad in bed.*

"Eric, just get a grip," says Bridget.

"Fine . . . I've now got a grip." He takes a phony deep breath. "And now I want an explanation!"

Bridget rolls her eyes and Caitlyn lights her cigarette, then purposely doesn't return the matches, hiding them in her purse. *And his paintings suck. Thank God I got these matches back.*

13

Kevin and Lucy are rather unsteadily walking up Third Street, headed for Monica's party. Kevin spies along the wall of the abandoned building at 21 East Third Street a number of posters. The posters show a photograph of a woman in a wedding dress attacking a bust of Sigmund Freud with an ax. The Rose Gallery on Greene Street will be presenting this performance in two weeks. Kevin stares at the poster; the woman in the bridal gown is his newly-minted ex-girlfriend Ellie.

"Oh, this is beautiful," says Kevin. "This is perfect. This is just what I fucking needed tonight. Do you believe this?" The posters disturb him on many levels: Ellie exists, Ellie exists without him, and Ellie exists quite successfully. Her art career is thriving. His sucks. She's winning.

Lucy looks at the posters. "It's Ellie," she says.

"Yeah, I know it's Ellie! See, she knew I'd be walking down this street tonight! That's why she deliberately put these flyers here." He goes right up to Ellie's image and shouts: "Well, it's not going to work, Ellie!"

"Kevin, Jesus—"

"You hear me, Ellie? I'm doing just fine without you! Just fine—you got that?"

"Oh, yeah," says Lucy, "you're doing great."

Kevin kicks the wall of the building and bruises his foot. "Perfect! This is perfect!" He turns back to Lucy. "Look, I've had it," he says. "This is bullshit. I'm going home to kill myself. Want to share a cab?"

"So I can pass out and wake up alone on New Year's Day? Forget it. I'm going to that party." She keeps walking, approaches Bowery. "I've got a date, remember?"

"A date?" Kevin asks, catching up to Lucy at the corner. He's limping noticeably after kicking 21 East Third. "What, you mean the bartender?"

"Of course I mean that bartender. You should come, too. Maybe you'll meet somebody."

"I refuse to buy into this desperation to find someone just because it's New Year's Eve. It's ridiculous and demeaning."

"Life is ridiculous and demeaning," says Lucy, and for a moment the profundity of her statement quiets their drunken minds. The truth of her remark is rather devastating, but only for a moment. Humans have a great capacity for denial and hope, and Lucy suddenly has an idea that gives her hope. "You know," she says, "you should have sex on your birthday."

"What is that, some kind of rule?" asks Kevin bitterly.

"Yeah, in fact . . ." She looks at Kevin, but she stops herself from saying what she thought of saying. *It's too crazy.* "No, forget it," she says, more to herself than to Kevin. They stand there on the corner of Bowery and Third Street, not moving.

"What? Forget what?" he asks, but he knows what she was going to say.

"Nothing."

Kevin looks at Lucy. *She wants me, I can't believe it.* He starts to get aroused. "Are you offering yourself to me, Lucy?"

"Well, I was going to say, you know, if this bartender thing doesn't work out . . ."

Kevin is hurt that now she's pretending to be ambivalent, falsely relegating him to second choice. "Yeah, right," he says dismissively.

"What? You think the bartender wouldn't go for me? You think I'm ugly or something?"

"No, I think you're drunk and deluded."

"You think I'm ugly."

"Lucy, you know I don't have ugly people for friends."

That's not what she wanted to hear. She made herself vulnerable, let him know that she'd like to have sex with him, and he lumps her into the category of all his friends. Why couldn't he just let her know that he thinks she's attractive? She realizes she never should have opened up to him. The booze is heightening everything. Bringing out truths and bringing out fears. She wants out. *I've got to get away from him.*

"You know something?" she says. "This is clearly a waste of time because you're just hell-bent on eliminating any trace of joy from this holiday!" She could almost cry. She's wanted Kevin for a long time and now it's out. *Nineteen eighty-two sucks and it's still 1981.* She starts back on Third Street the way they came.

"Where are you going?" Kevin calls after her.

"Away from you."

14

Monica is staring at Hillary. Hillary is sleeping on a chair. Monica slaps her friend on the head.

"What the hell—" says a groggy Hillary.

"Wake up," says Monica.

"What?"

"What time is it?" asks Monica.

Hillary wonders if Monica slapped her or if she dreamed that Monica slapped her. *Did that bitch slap me or did I just wake up and she was standing there?* She checks her wrist-watch. "It's 9:35."

"Nine thirty-five?"

"Yeah," yawns Hillary. She figures Monica didn't slap her. She's nuts, but not nuts enough to slap somebody who's sleeping.

"Nine thirty-five." Monica walks over to the window and stares down at the street. It's only four flights. *If I jumped out and died, they'd all feel bad. They'll all cry at my funeral. But if I just broke my leg, I'd be even more of a loser.* "Why do you think they're doing this to me, Hillary?"

Hillary gets up and pours herself another wine. "I don't know," she says.

Monica continues to stare out the window. "I think I'm finally reaching the point of acceptance, though. I mean, about no one showing up. It's kind of liberating, in a way, coming face to face with your worst nightmare. It's like facing death." She thinks about jumping. *Four flights.*

"For Christ's sake," says Hillary, "you're not facing death. It's just a stupid New Year's Eve party."

Monica looks at Hillary. "You're turning on me, too."

Hillary doesn't like Monica's tone and there's an odd gleam in her eye. *Maybe she did slap me awake. I'm out of here.* "That's it. I'm leaving." She grabs her purse and coat.

Monica races across the loft. "But you can't go—you're my only guest! You can't leave before midnight!"

"I'll be back later," says Hillary.

"No, you won't! You say you will, but you won't!"

Hillary ignores her. She's glad they don't work together anymore; she'd hate to have to see her at the office after this disaster. She walks to the door, grabs the handle.

Monica puts her body and weight against the door, something both of them have only seen in the movies. But in desperate moments, when we don't know what to do, life often does imitate the cinema. We need directions from somewhere.

"Hillary, please, don't leave me!" Monica begs. "Don't make me spend New Year's Eve all alone in here with the banners and the balloons and the crab dip! I can't take it!"

"Jesus, do you hear yourself?"

Hillary pulls open the door even with Monica against it. Monica, despite her neurosis about weight, isn't that heavy. Hillary gets through the threshold of the door and Monica grabs the strap of Hillary's purse.

"Cut the shit," says Hillary. They struggle with the strap. Hillary worries about it breaking, the purse is a Chanel from Bloomingdale's.

"Hillary, listen to me—you want to meet interesting guys, right? If you stay, I'll give you Eric!"

Hillary stops struggling. The combatants relax. Negotiations have begun. Diplomacy is at work. "Eric? Who's Eric?"

"You know—Eric. My last boyfriend."

"I don't believe I recall an Eric."

"Hillary, Jesus. We only broke up six months ago."

"Look, I don't remember who *I* was dating six months ago!"

Hillary tries to leave again; diplomacy has failed; Monica, resorting again to force, grabs Hillary's wrist. "You remember— *Eric.* He has a trust fund. He's a painter. We saw his show together."

Hillary's synapses start to form a connection: family money . . . paintings . . . dark curly hair . . . not bad looking.

Monica lets go of Hillary's wrist and continues to fill in the picture: "He does those abstracts with all the, uh . . ." She doesn't finish. If she reminds Hillary that Eric paints strange vaginas, Hillary might think he's a perv and leave. And Eric is her only bargaining chip.

"He paints flowers, right?" asks Hillary. Her memory is not that sharp, but she remembers the general shape of the images.

"Yeah, exactly," says Monica.

"He isn't seeing anyone?"

"No one worth mentioning."

Hillary weighs her options. "Okay. I'll do it."

"Thank God you'll stay. Come back in. Let's have another wine."

"No, I'm still leaving—but now I'll come back."

"You'll come back? What do you mean, you'll come back? We made a deal."

"I know . . . See, I wasn't coming back before, but now I will."

"But that's not our deal! Our deal is I give you Eric and you're not supposed to leave!"

"Well, this is the new deal! Okay? The new deal!" And before Monica can grab her again, Hillary, heels and all, runs down the stairs.

Monica closes the door and faces her empty, hellish apartment. She begins to cry. She thinks of gassing herself, but remembers that her stove is electric. *What if I put my head in the oven anyway? Maybe I'll electrocute myself.*

15

Eric and Bridget are standing in front of 21 East Third Street. Eric thought they were on their way to Monica's party, but Bridget was just mustering the courage to break up with him, and she just did, right in front of the poster of the ax-wielding Ellie. "Eric, I want to break up with you" was the clean and neat way she put it. Caitlyn is a few feet ahead, smoking a cigarette, thinking about how she has three hours to put her diaphragm to use. And it's a new one, too. She'd like to get her money's worth out of it.

Eric can't believe Bridget has dropped this bomb. "You're breaking up with me?"

"Yes."

"Because of some party? I told you, we broke up a long time ago."

"It's not just that. It's lots of things. We want different things. We're different kinds of people." Bridget is resorting to the standard-issue breakup remarks.

"Different kinds of people? What the hell does that mean?"

"Things just aren't working out," she says, trying the direct but civil approach now.

"Well, I don't know what to say. I thought everything was fine." He's hurt. For him this is coming out of nowhere.

Bridget is sensing the need for a good lie, the guy seems to be in pain. She feels a little bad. "Look, to tell you the truth," she says, lying, "I'm still in love with my old boyfriend."

"Your old boyfriend?" Eric smells the condescending lie. A lie to make him feel better, but such lies only kick you when you're down. He eyes Bridget, looking for a slipup in her face, something that reveals that she's bluffing. He has to check because there's the outside possibility that she's telling the truth. But he can't read her one way or the other. She has too good a poker face. So he presses her to reveal her hand. "But you never mentioned this," he says. "You never mentioned an old boyfriend."

"Well, I have one, okay?" She's exasperated. This breakup is taking too long.

"He's French Canadian," says Caitlyn, wanting to help out. Lend the lie some color.

"Yeah. I met him while I was . . . camping," says Bridget. She pictures a tent, a handsome Canuck. She kind of likes this fantasy.

"I don't believe this," says Eric. These girls are kicking him in the balls, then kicking him in the teeth.

"See, we never even officially broke up. He just . . . disappeared one day on a mountain climbing trip."

"Everyone thought he was dead," says Caitlyn. The two friends are on the same wavelength.

"But this morning he called, so . . ." Bridget trails off, running out of fictions. She's not that imaginative.

Eric helps her out. "So he just called you up, out of the blue—just called to say he isn't dead."

"That's right," says Bridget.

"This is the most ridiculous story I've ever heard in my entire life!" says Eric, and he's livid, kicking at the ground, pacing back and forth in tight little steps. He could explode.

"Jesus, Eric. Calm down," says Bridget.

"What kind of person are you, anyway—just blurting it out like this—just breaking up with me in the street on New Year's Eve?" He stares at the poster of Ellie with the ax. He'd like to have an ax.

"Sorry," says Bridget, without much feeling.

"Oh, you're sorry? Yeah, well . . . you better be sorry! Because you're the one who has to live with this, not me! You're the one inventing old boyfriends and bringing them back from the dead." He spies Caitlyn taking all this in, getting a kick out of it. "And you," he says to her, thinking of the matchbook, "with your sordid little agenda. Well, I've had it with both of you! You deserve each other." He storms off in the direction of Bowery. "You think I need this?" he exclaims over his shoulder. "Let me tell you something—I don't need this!"

"Do you believe him?" asks Bridget.

"*Really,*" says Caitlyn. "Like it's *your* fault he's bad in bed."

16

Val and Stephie are at a pay phone at the corner of Sixth Street and Avenue B; there were phones on Fourth Street and Fifth Street, but they didn't work. It is one of the banes of a New Yorker's existence that, invariably, when you really need to make a call, pay phone after pay phone will be broken. You will lose money continuously, though on occasion a phone will unexpectedly yield quite a bit of change, like a slot machine. It is a guilty pleasure when this happens. But overall, when it comes to gambling with New York City pay phones, one loses far more than one wins. The House always comes out ahead.

So Val is calling her mother. Across the avenue from the two Ronkonkoma natives is a punk-rock bar known as the Ugly Dog, which is where the four young men who had terrorized Stephie were heading. And more patrons of the bar, with their wild hairdos and studded belts and unhealthy pallors, are streaming into the club, which vibrates with the noise—rather, the music—of the band inside. Stephie stares at these punk rock creatures with awe and horror. *Don't they have mothers? How do they sleep with those hair spikes coming out of their head?*

Val hangs up the phone. "There's no answer."

"Oh, my God—there's no answer? What's your fucking mother doing not answering her phone?"

"I don't know. Maybe she went to a party or something."

Stephie is certain now that she'll be raped. Possibly by several punk rockers with daggerlike hairdos. "This is the worst night," says Stephie.

"Maybe my mother's just down in the laundry room," says Val, wanting to defreak the freaked-out Stephie, give her some hope.

"Look, please—just call that band and tell them we're meeting them early, okay?" pleads Stephie, and she takes the phone off the hook and passes it to Val, who promptly hangs it back up.

"I can't make that call," says Val.

"What do you mean, you can't?"

"Because I just can't, okay?"

Stephie stares at her and then realizes something truly horrific.

"Oh, my God! There isn't any band, is there?"

"What are you talking about?"

"I'm talking about you—the liar—who's been bragging for months how we're hanging out with a band in the Village on New Year's Eve—when really there ain't no band, there ain't no nothing!"

Val who prides herself on being cool, above it all, and most of all cooler than Stephie, in charge of Stephie, breaks down and confesses the truth.

"Well, it was the only way I could get you to come to the city with me!" she says. Val knows how much Stephie loves bands, and so lying about a band was the best way to get her to come to New York, because you couldn't just go to New York to meet guys by yourself, you need a friend. You need a Stephie.

"I bet your cousin isn't even having a party! I bet you made the whole story up!"

"She is having a party, I just need the right address." Val looks across the street to the Ugly Dog. "Look, let's just go in there. We'll get a couple beers and try my mother again later."

"Val, we don't belong in there! We don't belong on fucking B! We're in way over our heads here!"

"Stephie, we got money and we got fake ID's. From where I'm standing, we got just as much right to be in there as anybody else."

Stephie happens to glance over Val's shoulder. Two men are approaching. It's the two guys in leather jackets again. Stephie is sure that they've been following her and Val, and then one of the guys points at them and says something to his partner. Stephie tries to tell Val what's happening, but her tongue is paralyzed again. The poor girl is aging twenty years tonight.

"What? What's wrong?" asks Val.

Stephie clutches her friend. "Val, it's those guys!" She begins to whisper. "I saw them before. They're following us."

"Are they cute?"

"Val!"

"I'm just asking!"

"Just, come on, okay?" says Stephie, and, holding on to Val, she runs across the street and into the Ugly Dog. Stephie, like a voter on election day, feels that she has been forced to choose between two evils. She opts, in her mind, for being raped in the punk-rock bar as opposed to on the street by the men in the leather jackets.

What Stephie could really use this night is a good old-fashioned chastity belt. One made of steel with a vault-like combination lock and a car alarm. This might make her feel a bit more secure. Also a gun, a mace, and a police whistle would be helpful.

17

Kevin catches up to Lucy after their fight over her clumsy proposition, and he convinces her that they should go to the Kiev, to eat some heavy Ukrainian food and sober up.

So they sit by the window in the back of the Kiev, a narrow restaurant famous for its good prices and large portions. A sturdy Russian waitress takes their order and gives them some challah bread to eat while they wait. The challah soaks up some of the alcohol in their stomachs, and so they eat the bread and smoke cigarettes and sit there rather silently. Lucy thinks about what she said to Kevin and she can't believe Kevin didn't jump on her offer, and Kevin thinks about what it would be like to jump off the George Washington Bridge into the Hudson, but it's an idea he disregards because he doesn't like pain and he hated swimming in cold pools as a child.

Then the waitress sets before the two friends a plate of steaming, fried cottage-cheese-and-potato blintzes. They look like rolled-up yellow napkins that you eat.

Lucy takes a bite and then says to Kevin, "I can't even tell you how many men I've fucked." She blurts this out, still feeling the need to convince Kevin of her desirability in the eyes of other men.

"I believe you," says Kevin.

"I mean, I couldn't even make a list, that's how many there are."

"Lucy, I believe that you've fucked many, many men. Okay? Can we drop it now?" He doesn't like to imagine his friend spreading her legs for a legion of jerks.

"A lot more than Ellie, that's for sure. She's too busy making trivial performance art to attract anyone, except you—oh, and Jack, of course."

Kevin, who is compulsively cutting up a blintz, looks up. "What? Jack?"

"But then, you know Jack—he'll fuck anybody."

"Jack . . . and Ellie? Jack the actor? I think I saw him back at the bar, right before we left. He was walking to the pool table in the back with a cute girl . . . The bastard. He's a male slut. When did this happen? When did he sleep with Ellie?"

"I don't know, a few—a few weeks ago. A month." She puts a big mouthful of cottage-cheese blintz in her mouth; it's mildly sobering.

"You mean this happened recently? While we were still together? Why didn't you tell me?" His breakup wound seems to be getting more infected as the night goes on. First the poster and now the news that she was cheating on him. Even

61

when he thought things were good, they were bad. He can't even have any fond memories. He was a cuckold and didn't know it. That makes him a retroactive cuckold.

"I thought you knew," says Lucy. "Everybody else did."

"I don't believe this. I think my life sucks and then I find out it sucks more."

"Ellie's appeal is this whole Zelda thing, right?" Lucy asks, trying to figure out why Kevin ever liked her.

Kevin doesn't answer. He leans his head back and covers his face with his napkin. He is withdrawing from the world. A world he can no longer be a part of.

Lucy ignores this napkin maneuver and continues on her Zelda theme: "She gets men because she makes them miserable, right? She always has you wondering if she really likes you, so you're always chasing her, trying to please her, but it makes you feel like shit. But a lot of guys, like you, must want that. You know, to feel like shit."

Kevin speaks through his napkin, as through a veil of tears. "Yes, we like to feel like shit. It reminds us of childhood. I feel like shit right now. So I have to say, this is turning out to be an even worse birthday than I expected. I wasn't expecting much, but this . . . this is an unprecedented low."

The napkin falls off his face and onto his lap, where it belongs. He wipes his hands on it and stares at the ugly yellow blintzes.

Lucy eyeballs him. The blintzes are sobering her up a little, but she still has her drunken anger. "Look," she says. "Don't try to make me feel sorry for you. First you tell me not to mention your birthday, but then you whine about it, so I buy you a present. A whole carton of cigarettes, which you promptly lose. So you are not allowed to feel self-pity about your birthday. You're not even allowed to feel self-pity about Ellie anymore because that whole relationship was set up to fail. Okay? So one more whine out of you and I won't speak to you for the first six months of '82."

Kevin doesn't say anything. He's with a friend who can't stand him, who earlier had offered to give him sex for his birthday. Nothing makes sense.

Lucy forks a piece of blintz and points it at Kevin and some of the lumpy bright white cottage cheese falls out of the blintz and onto the plate like a thick gob of snow. Kevin watches it fall and feels mildly nauseated, but doesn't say anything. He's on complaining probation. "And I'll tell you something else," Lucy says, jabbing the piece of forked blintz in a threatening way, "you're going to that party with me whether you like it or not. And you just better pray to God that bartender shows up. One of us has to have a good time tonight, and it's going to be me."

18

Back at Jack Dempsey's, Jack gives the quarterback-bartender twenty dollars for the chandelier. He does this despite Cindy's protests that she'll pay for it, but Jack won't let her; he feels obligated to do the chivalrous thing. She's secretly touched by this and Jack's secretly miffed.

They leave the bar and when they get outside, Cindy says, "I'm really sorry, that was really embarrassing. . . . Do you think that wine stain will ever come out of the pool table?" She gives a little giggle after her question to try to make light of things.

"Probably not," Jack says without much humor. "But I wasn't planning on ever going there again, anyway." He says this attempting to be playfully sarcastic, but the result is cutting, revealing his underlying dissatisfaction with how their evening has been going.

"Look, maybe I should just go home," Cindy says. Beyond the debacle in Jack Dempsey's, the two of them are simply not getting along. She's just too nervous tonight and it's making both of them uncomfortable.

"Well, if that's what you really want to do," Jack says, relieved. "I'll get you a cab, then."

He steps out into the avenue to flag down a taxi. Cindy stands on the curb beside him.

"Maybe we could do this another time," says Cindy.

"Sure, sure," says Jack. He looks for a free taxi, but they're all taken.

"You know, we could have another date when there isn't so much pressure."

"That sounds good," says Jack, distractedly. He just wants to spot a cab.

"Like I said before, I feel a lot of pressure because of the New Year's Eve date thing and I . . . Well, I don't usually do the kind of thing I did last night."

A cab goes by. "Taxi," Jack calls out, even though there are people in the back seat. Sometimes you just have to call out "Taxi," even when you know the taxi won't stop. It's like pushing the button on an elevator more than once. You have to do *something.* "Goddamn it!" says Jack. He wants to get this girl a cab.

"In fact, to be perfectly honest," says Cindy, but then she hesitates—should she tell him? But Jack is hardly listening to her anyway, his male mind is focused on the goal at hand—

hailing a cab. But then she comes out with it. She feels that he should know why she's been acting so weird. "You know—last night—what happened," she says. "I had never done it before."

This gets through to Jack. Is she saying what he thinks she is saying? He turns to her, taking his eye off the road, possibly missing a chance at a taxi. "Did what?" he asks.

"You know—*it.*"

"You never did *it?*" *Oh, my God, I had sex with a virgin and I didn't even realize it. I didn't see any blood. There's supposed to be blood.*

"Well . . . no," says Cindy, and she puts her finger in her mouth and chews her nail.

Jack steps back onto the sidewalk, to be next to her. "Why didn't you tell me?" he asks.

"I guess I was afraid you'd think I was a freak or something." Cindy, who's twenty-four, doesn't have a single friend who has waited as long as she.

"So what you're saying is . . . I was your first?" Jack likes this. What man doesn't like to be first? First at everything. First to the moon. First to the North Pole. First to the South Pole. First in home runs. A girl's first lover.

"Yes, you were my first," Cindy says to Jack, looking down at her feet in a sweet way.

"So I was the first guy you ever let . . ."

"Yeah."

Jack is quiet. This is a spiritual moment for him. Something beautiful happened last night and he didn't know it at the time, but he knows it now. Every guy wants to sleep with a virgin at least once, and now he has it on his lovemaking résumé. What Cindy did is give him the best compliment in the world and Jack loves compliments. "Wow," he says.

"Jack, you're embarrassing me." She smiles at him. She likes him. She doesn't know why, but she really likes him. She gave him her virginity.

"I'm sorry, it's just . . . I don't know what to say. I'm stunned. This has never happened to me before."

"Well, now you know how I feel," Cindy says.

"But . . . why me? I mean, we hardly knew each other . . ."

"I don't know, it's kind of weird to talk about it on the street, okay?" she says, and then she sneezes. It's cold out. Jack protectively puts his arm around her. This sweet little doll who chose him to be her first.

"Sure, sure. I understand," he says. "Look, it's freezing out here. Let's get you inside, okay? You must be hungry." There's no reason why she should be hungry, but he feels that she's undergone a major physical trauma and must need food, and he wants to provide food for his little ex-virgin. He wants to take care of her.

"You don't want me to go home?" she asks.

"No, no, no. Let's get you some food. We can go to the party later."

"You're sure?"

"Sure I'm sure . . . Let's go to the Little India street, you know, Sixth Street. There's a ton of restaurants. You like Indian?"

"Oh. Well, sure. I mean, if you do." She's lapsing back into indecisiveness, but now it doesn't bother Jack. *I slept with a virgin.* He keeps his arm around her and walks her toward Little India.

19

Bridget and Caitlyn are back at Jack Dempsey's after the breakup with Eric. Bridget is flirting with the quarterback-bartender. She likes him, and he likes her. He likes redheads. His first girlfriend had freckles just like Bridget. He decides to invite her and Caitlyn to the party that Lucy told him about. Monica's party.

"I know this party," he says. "I hear it's going to be pretty good. I'm getting off in a little while if you guys are interested. Just let me know."

"Thanks, we will," says Bridget, unaware of course that he's just invited them to the very party they're still planning on going to, even though the host is the ex-girlfriend of Bridget's now–ex-boyfriend, Eric.

The bartender goes to the other end of the bar. The big Irishman and many others need drinks.

"He is so cute," says Bridget.

"How can you waste your time on idle flirtation when it's like almost ten on New Year's Eve and neither of us has a date?" She's pissed off that the bartender has been paying attention to Bridget. *I can't believe he's attracted to her and not me. Her freckles are gross. I better take my coat off so he can see my chest.*

"What's wrong with the bartender?" asks Bridget, while Caitlyn puts her coat on the back of her bar stool.

"Please. It's too desperate getting picked up by some bartender."

"'Some bartender.' What are you? You're a waitress."

"Excuse me—I'm an artist."

"So maybe he's an artist, too."

"Bridget, I promise you, he is not an artist. He's much too cute. He's an ex-jock. And now he's an actor. What else could he be? A dumb actor, ex-jock."

"So being cute automatically means you're stupid or something?"

"Look, you can't count on guys who are that cute, okay?" says Caitlyn. She doesn't want Bridget getting lucky unless she's getting lucky at the same time. She has to pop Bridget's balloon pronto. "Cute guys are fucked up in ways normal-looking people can't even imagine."

This strikes Bridget as a truth, so she feels a little demoralized about the bartender and she says, "I shouldn't have broken up with Eric."

"Will you forget him? We've still got two hours."

"Listen, Caitlyn, I know a girl who went home alone on New Year's Eve and it's like she was jinxed for the whole year. For twelve months, she was invisible to guys. It's like she was tainted."

This spooks Caitlyn. Her new diaphragm cost more than a hundred dollars. What if it doesn't fit twelve months from now? She doesn't have that kind of money to burn. "We're getting dates, okay?" she says with the urgency of a soldier in a foxhole reassuring another soldier that they'll make it home someday. "When have we ever not gotten dates on New Year's Eve?"

"It happened to me—remember? In '78? That time I went home alone?"

"Excuse me, as I recall you were in a committed monogamous relationship that week."

"There was no committed monogamous relationship. That was just a cover story."

Caitlyn looks at her, shocked. She can't believe Bridget lied to her three years ago. "So you were the one who was jinxed for a whole year!"

"I can't believe I let you talk me into breaking up with Eric!"

Caitlyn lights a cigarette rather than talk about the Eric issue.

So Bridget sucks some ice out of her drink and munches on it nervously and this upsets her. *Oh, my God, I'm chewing on ice. That means I'm already sexually frustrated. I may already be jinxed.*

She spits out her ice and lights a cigarette. She and Caitlyn smoke and look at themselves in the mirror behind the bar. It doesn't occur to Bridget that smoking, with all its oral implications, might also be a sign of sexual frustration.

20

Monica is alone in her apartment watching TV. *Love Story,* with Ryan O'Neal and Ali MacGraw, is playing. Ryan and Ali are holding hands and walking along a perfect tree-lined New England street, and they are looking very happy and very much in love and very perfect. They wear very beautiful sweaters.

This picture is too much for our devastated hostess.

"I hate you, you motherfuckers," Monica shouts, and she throws her wineglass at this image of love and the wine fizzes against the TV screen. Just then the doorbell rings. Monica sits up. Could it be?

She turns off the volume on the TV, but leaves the picture on so the loft has some people in it, and she runs to the door. "Guests!" she exclaims. "Thank you, God! Oh, thank you, thank you, thank you." She flings open the door. It's Eric, her ex-boyfriend of six months ago. Not the perfect guest, but she throws her arms around him nonetheless.

"Eric! Hi! Happy New Year!"

Eric looks past Monica and sees the empty, barren, and depressing loft. "Oh, great party," he says.

Monica makes light of this. "It's nothing," she says. "No one wants to be the first to arrive, that's all." She takes his arm and leads him to the drink and food table before he can leave.

"How about something to eat? You want something to eat?" She lifts up the crab dip, proffering it to him. "I made it myself," she says.

Eric grabs a chip and plunges it into the crab dip. He eats the chip violently, and then scoops out a big thing of salsa onto another chip. Then he pours himself a drink. Then he makes a mess of the guacamole dip. He's taking out his frustration about the breakup with Bridget on Monica's dips. Monica tries to ignore this. *I have a guest. I have a guest. Be grateful or God will take him away.*

She tries to make conversation. "So where's what's-her-name?" If Eric's new girlfriend is coming she'll have two guests, but that's the worst question she could ask.

"She's not coming," he says, and then he violently shoves a chip deep into the guacamole. There are now unseemly craters in all her dips and dip drippings on the table. Eric is making a pig of himself.

"How come she's not coming?" asks Monica.

"She broke up with me! Do you believe that? Here it is New Year's Eve and she breaks up with me!"

Monica barely hears this news. She's distracted by the mess

Eric has made. Her food table is in a shambles after only one guest. She begins to straighten up. If other people do arrive she wants it to look nice.

Eric takes a sip of his drink and says, "And you wouldn't believe the story she comes up with! Suddenly she's got this mountain climber boyfriend everybody thought was dead—but now it turns out he's alive, so she's going back to him. Have you ever heard such shit? It's humiliating."

He'd like Monica, an ex, to maybe comfort him a little. But all she's doing is cleaning up the table and smoothing out the dips, as if to erase any evidence of his being there.

"Yeah, well," Monica says in an offhand manner, "you know how it is." She's being brusque because she has her own worries. *Got to get him away from the food.* "Say, you know what we need? We need some music. Don't you think? Come with me to the stereo."

She takes his arm and leads him away from the food and over to the record player. "Something Christmassy?" she suggests.

"I hate Christmas," says Eric.

"Jesus, Eric. Lighten up. It's the holidays. We have to play holiday music. And anyway, Bridget is a bimbo." She selects a record. Bing Crosby's "White Christmas." *There's no way he can't like this, everybody likes this.*

Bing comes on and Eric says, "God, I hate the holidays . . . and I hate Bridget and I hate this song!" And the whole night begins to rise up inside Eric like a geyser. The sitting in the bar while the two girls had their twenty-minute conference in the toilet; the bizarro matchbook with Caitlyn's number; the shattering of that chandelier over the pool table, it almost gave him a heart attack; and then the incredibly rude breakup by Bridget—on New Year's Eve! And now a fucking party with nobody present except his ex-girlfriend, and fucking Bing Crosby singing. Then Eric sees Ryan O'Neal's loathsome, preppy, handsome face on the TV, and so, like an aneurysm bursting, Eric suddenly and unexpectedly throws his wineglass with great fury at the screen. "It's all bullshit!" he shouts, in primal agony.

The wine fizzes against the screen, the plastic cup bounces off, indestructible. And Monica takes this all in, but isn't upset. She's more intrigued by the fact that another person felt compelled to throw a wineglass at *Love Story*. She feels, momentarily, less alone in the world.

21

Val and Stephie are in the crowded punk bar, the Ugly Dog. The music is deafening and the smoke is as thick as horror-film fog. Stephie is afraid to bump into somebody and maybe lose an eye on a hair spike. Val is trying to get close to the bar, but it is hard to make headway. She waves at the bartender, but he doesn't see her.

"Hey!" she screams over the music, through the smoke. "Can we get some beers over here?"

Stephie is so nervous that she has to use the bathroom, but she's afraid to. Even if she covered the seat with lots of toilet paper she probably could get something. *I'm just going to have to hold it, probably until we're back in Ronkonkoma.*

Val screams again at the bartender, but to no effect. Then Stephie spots the two guys from outside. The huge leather-jacket guys. They've come in the bar and again they point at Val and Stephie. They're shoving their way through the crowd to the two girls.

"Val, we have to go," says Stephie.

"Will you give me a second? I just want to get us some beer."

"But Val, it's them. Those guys. They're coming right for us."

Val sees the guys and since Stephie has convinced her that they are dangerous, she and Stephie start pushing to the back of the bar, hoping to find a rear exit. The two guys are following, but the bar is so packed that their progress is slow. Stephie and Val cut through the dance floor at the rear of the bar, and they get a little roughed up, since the punks are slam-dancing, but Stephie and Val come out the other side and see a back door.

"There's a door," shouts Stephie, fighting for her life, fighting for her hymen.

They open this door and sure enough, there's an alleyway. They race down this alleyway, thinking freedom is theirs, but at the end of the narrow, garbage-can–laden path, there is a high chain-link fence with razor wire at the top.

"We're fucked!" howls Stephie.

"Oh my God . . . I can't breathe," says Val, who is mildly asthmatic.

Then they see the back door of the club open up. A plume of cigarette smoke first appears, then the two huge guys. The girls huddle together against the fence. The leather jackets approach. Stephie whispers into Val's ear: "I told you we were gonna get raped on B! It happens all the time down here."

Both girls close their eyes and wait for the inevitable. Val, despite her asthma, has a little fight in her and she whispers to Stephie, "When they're about to do it, try to kick them in the balls. I saw it in a movie. It's our only chance."

The two leather-jackets stand in front of the poor, frightened Long Island girls. With her eyes closed, Stephie yells what may be her last words: "Fuck you!"

The taller of the two rapists, Tom, is not fazed by this. "How you doing?" he asks. "Kind of hot back in there, isn't it?"

The girls don't answer. They keep their eyes closed. Dave, Tom's buddy, who has a large gut, finishes eating a hot dog that he has with him, and underneath his jacket is something large and bulky. Tom tries again with the huddled girls.

"We thought we'd come outside and get some air," he says. "You know, take the opportunity to introduce ourselves or something." Tom speaks quite well, almost softly, and he's not bad looking. He has a strong chin with a week's beard on it and he has a thick head of dark brown hair. Dave is less attractive. He has a double chin with two weeks' growth of beard, and his gut is rather sloppy and unappealing.

The girls open their big, frightened eyes. Tom takes this as a good sign. "I'm Tom," he says. "And this is Dave."

Dave grunts hello. He feels a burning in his belly from the hot dog. He'd like to burp but he doesn't want to piss Tom off. Then Tom hits Dave, and says, "Where's your manners? Show the girls what we got for 'em."

Dave begins to unzip his leather jacket. Stephie feels her bladder about to explode. *He's going to take out a gun and shoot us and rape us when we're dead. Or rape us, then shoot us.*

Dave removes a six-pack of beer. Stephie exhales, and Val is psyched. *Finally some beer.* At this time in her life, Val is a simple person. She has only two interests: boys and beer, especially as the two seem to go together.

"Bevo," says Dave. "Bevo," in his vocabulary, means beverages. And he smiles proudly, holding up the beer, like he's a triumphant caveman proffering to the cavewomen gathered around the clan's fire a fresh kill, some meat, food. And for practical reasons, beyond manly provider reasons, he's glad to produce the six-pack: He could use a beer to calm down that hot dog, which is setting off gas in his large belly.

"Join us?" asks Tom.

"Definitely," says Val.

Stephie would rather not, but her nerves are too frayed to offer a protest. She just wishes she could click her heels and go home, but she can't. And to make things worse, she's about to pee in her pants. She'd like to go home just to use her home toilet. "I have to pee," she says, sadly, forlornly. She can't hold it any longer. So the four go back into the bar, and Stephie heads to the ladies' room. She goes into the stall. There's not even any toilet paper for layering the seat a hundred times over. This is the worst night of her life, by far. But she's adaptable. *I'll stand on the toilet and squat, that's how I'll do it.*

22

Kevin and Lucy have finished their blintzes and now they are eating pierogis. Lucy takes the last bite of a pierogi, a greasy pillow-shaped potato dumpling, and then she lights a cigarette. She stares at Kevin. She's sobering up, but she still has plenty of *in vino veritas* left. She can't help but speak the truth. And the truth is she wants to have sex with Kevin. She wants to have more than sex with Kevin. She wants him to be her boyfriend, but this desire is still subconscious. Right now she just wants him to want her, she needs it for her ego.

"Kevin," she says calmly. "We've done enough fighting. This practically makes us lovers. Let's go have sex."

"I don't want to," he says. He eats a pierogi. He doesn't want to have sex with Lucy because she's his friend and he knows many of the guys she has slept with. They aren't faceless, like when you go out with somebody whose whole sexual history is a mystery to you, which is how men prefer things to be. As long as your girlfriend's ex-lovers are faceless they don't haunt you, it's almost like they don't exist. You delude yourself into thinking, basically, that you are your woman's only lover, ever. That she was for all intents and purposes a virgin when you met, especially since no man ever made love to her as well as you do. Therefore, by virtue of your superior lovemaking, you cancel out the past. You are a revelation. Men need to do this because of their intrinsic competitiveness and their intrinsic insecurity, which are, naturally, related.

Therefore, since Kevin has been a friend and confidant to Lucy, he knows many of her lovers—not all, but many—and so if he started making love with her, he knows that he might start visualizing all her ex-boyfriends that he has met doing it with her. It would be harder for him to delude himself into feeling like he's Lucy's one and only lover. So that's why he won't have sex with her.

"Why don't you want to?" she asks, completely unaware of the convoluted male logic behind his refusal.

"Would you please just drop this and let me enjoy my pierogis? They're the only thing giving me pleasure in this whole night."

"I won't drop this. I have a right to know as your friend why you won't fuck me!"

Kevin puts down his fork. His beloved pierogi. "Look," he says. "You really want to fuck? Because if you really, really want to, Lucy, we'll fuck. Okay?"

He figures that this should call her bluff, and she'll drop the whole thing and they can eat their pierogis, then drink more, then start the miserable new year with a sickening hangover. That seems to him like a reasonable plan.

"You don't think I'm serious, do you?" she asks.

She's deranged by booze and New Year's Eve mania, he surmises, but he will try to reason with her. "How long have we known each other?" he asks.

"What?"

"In the five years that we've known each other, have you ever once considered having sex with me? I mean, before tonight?"

"You think I'm not attracted to you."

"Lucy, we both know you're not attracted to half the men you sleep with."

"What, now you think I'm a slut?"

She almost got him with that one, but he keeps a good poker face. "What?" he asks, laughing it off.

"That's what it is—that's why you won't do it. You think I'm a slut."

"Look—I don't think you're a slut, okay? Now keep your voice down." And really he doesn't think she's a *slut* slut, but knowing whom she has slept with does make her seem *easy,* and like most men he thinks that all women should be chaste, unless they are with him, then it's all right if they have sex and *want* sex. That's what gets most men—it's scary to think that women want sex. Sexual independence of women causes men great anxiety. Whole religions are set up to free men of this anxiety.

"I won't keep my voice down," she says, and then she blurts out, for all to hear, "YOU'RE SCARED TO HAVE SEX WITH ME! That's what it is, isn't it? Not that I'm a slut, but that you're scared."

Several of the other diners glance at Kevin and Lucy. The women are on Kevin's side and the men are on Lucy's. The men look at Lucy, with her dyed blond hair and cute face and good figure, and think to themselves, *She's a babe, I wouldn't be scared, I'd be delighted.* And the women think, *She's drunk, she should keep her voice down, no wonder he's scared.*

But Lucy, in accusing Kevin of cowardice, has hit on the other crucial reason men don't like to sleep with women who are friends. To not get an erection or to have an early misfire with a person who was formerly a friend and now is a woman (i.e., a female you are having sex with) is utterly humiliating. To exhibit a lack of sexual prowess with someone you used to be on equal footing with is terrible, even worse than having sexual dysfunction with a woman you are just getting to know. Every man wants to be a slugger the first time he comes to the plate, but he often isn't, and a man doesn't want a friend to know that he has feet of clay, a cock of clay.

"You think I'm afraid?"

"Please. It's so obvious."

"That's ridiculous."

"Oh, yeah? Prove it."

"Listen, I don't have to prove anything to you or anybody."

"Come on, Kevin," Lucy says, leaning in close to him, hovering over his pierogis. "I dare you. I dare you to fuck me. Fuck me right here in the Kiev."

This is a battle of the sexes over what they usually battle about: sex. That's why it's called a battle of the sexes. And this one is a real championship fight.

"So what are you saying?" Kevin retorts. "You want to have sex in a disgusting coffee shop bathroom? Is that what you want? Loveless New Year's sex with the stench of air freshener in your nose?"

"I guess you're too chicken to find out," Lucy says, and she takes a pierogi and bites it castratingly in two, then adds, "Or maybe you're just too broken up about Ellie and Jack."

She's verbally punched Kevin in the balls. But he grabs his balls and rises to the occasion. "All right," he says. "Stop eating that pierogi. We're going to the bathroom and I'm going to fuck you."

Lucy smiles and stands up. She's won round one.

They head to the bathroom for round two.

23

Jack and Cindy are eating at Gandhi II. Sitar music wails from unseen speakers, and the whole place is gaudily lit up with hundreds of flashing Christmas lights, along the walls and ceiling. But such lighting is not seasonal—in Gandhi II it is Christmas every day of the year. The bulbs are a permanent attraction, whether it's December and bitterly cold out or July and cruelly humid (the usual New York weather extremes). It is not a large restaurant; it's quite narrow, like many on Little India street; there are only about a dozen tables.

Cindy is enjoying her tandoori chicken, while Jack has barely touched his shrimp biryani. He's too busy staring at her. His virgin. His lovely trophy.

But Cindy doesn't like this staring. "Jack, please stop looking at me like that," she says.

"Sorry," Jack says, and he makes an effort to eat a shrimp, but then adds, "It's just that . . . what can I say? This is turning out to be a very unusual night."

"Unusual how?"

"No particular way . . . I do hate to press a point, but it's just, you know, I was wondering about what you said about last night being your first time and everything . . ."

"What about it?"

"Well, it's just I can't help wondering why me? I mean, what was it about me—in particular—that made you decide to, you know . . ."

Jack's ego can hardly take it, can hardly wait. He wants to hear why him. He's dying for the praise, even though he happens to be a man who gets praised by women a great deal. But he's a sponge for praise—he's an actor, after all. They need praise more than they need food. Without it they shrivel up and lose their looks, their reason for living. And Jack is a typical actor. He can't be complimented enough, and what Cindy has to say will be *new* praise. Something about himself that he hasn't heard before. After all, he's never been praised by a woman who chose him for her deflowering.

"Oh, right," says Cindy. "Well, let's see . . . why did I choose you?" She's silent, trying to come up with an answer. Jack is riveted, a big happy smile is on his face. He's so excited, his ego hungry like a dog at the table waiting for a real good scrap. But Cindy doesn't come through. "Sorry," she says, "I'm drawing a blank." And she digs back into her tandoori chicken, not realizing how this young man across from her is desperate for information. It's not enough that she gave him her cherry, he wants more. But he tries to hide this, save face.

"Oh, well, you know, that's fine. It's just . . . as an actor, I find myself intrigued by people's motivations." He attempts to eat his biryani, but he can't let it go. His dog-ego is a persistent beggar. So he tries again. "I mean, let's face it, you're an attractive girl," he says. "You must have had lots of opportunities. I mean, college alone. A guy's got to wonder, what makes him so great?"

"Well," Cindy begins, while still chewing her food, "one thing about last night that I remember was thinking you were probably the most—" But she is unable to continue, she has bitten down on a chili. She may as well have swallowed a lit cigarette. Her eyes bulge and water.

Jack, oblivious to her distress, only aware of his ego distress, pushes her to continue. "What? I was the most what?!?"

"Oh my God. Oh . . . Oh, no." Cindy doesn't want to, it's too humiliating, but she spits out her chewed-up food—like a cat vomiting—onto the plate, which serves as an odd answer to Jack's question.

"Are you all right?" Jack asks. No girl ever spit out her food in front of him. She's just sitting there, holding her mouth, her eyes welling with tears; her mouth is still on fire. "Drink some water," Jack advises. She lifts her glass and gulps some water, but in her hurry she spills most of it onto the front of her white cocktail dress, further smearing the lipstick stains that she collected in the bathroom at Jack Dempsey's.

"You must've eaten a chili," Jack says.

"It was so big . . . I thought it was a piece of chicken." She takes another gulp of water. Her mouth burns and then she suddenly feels a pain down in her groin, a burning twinge, a soreness from last night. She feels like she's on the verge of hysteria. Her mouth is on fire and her crotch is on fire. She wants to go hide in the bathroom and maybe cry while sitting on the john. So she abruptly stands up, and her chair, weighted down by her heavy winter coat, falls backward onto the floor. She whirls around to lift up the chair and knocks right into their short, bald waiter. Unfortunately, he happens to be carrying a platter of food, which goes flying onto the floor.

Jack watches it all in disbelief and the waiter curses under his breath and Cindy responds by bursting into tears—poor girl—and screaming, "Oh, God, I'm sorry!" She says this as if she is apologizing for many sins, and then she runs to the bathroom, which seems to be her *modus operandi* after causing disasters. Jack wonders if he'll have to pay for the food. He's already paid for the chandelier. The bald waiter squats down, it hurts his back, and he begins to clean up.

"Do I have to pay for this?" asks Jack.

24

Stephie has climbed onto the toilet and her pants and panties are at her ankles. Very slowly now, she begins to squat. She's in place. She relaxes and begins to pee. Relief. A moment of relief in a night of terror. She sighs. But then the bathroom door opens and the sudden infusion of noise startles her. The woman who has just come in, not seeing feet on the floor, rattles the stall handle. The lock holds. The woman rattles the door again. Stephie finishes peeing, but she's panicked, and when she tries to quickly pull up her panties, her foot slips and goes into the bowl! And she hasn't flushed.

"Fuck me!" she screams, and in a moment of great athletic heroism, befitting an Olympic gymnast, Stephie yanks her foot out of the toilet water and leaps, with pants still at ankles, off the toilet and onto the narrow strip of floor in front of the toilet. In moments of crisis, human beings are often capable of great feats of strength and agility.

"Fuck me! Fuck me! Fuck me!"

"Yeah, fuck you," says the woman who would like to use the toilet.

Stephie pulls up her pants and looks at her wet boot. *It's all Val's fault. I hate Val.*

She goes back out to the bar, and Tom and Dave and Val are in a corner drinking the beers. Tom and Dave bought the beers at the bodega on Third Street, but the bar is so crowded that they don't get hassled for not purchasing the club's booze. While Stephie was in the bathroom, Dave quickly chugged three beers, Tom had two, and Val is just finishing hers. That leaves no beers for Stephie, who hides her wet boot behind her dry boot.

Tom declares that they need more beer, and that it's cheaper at the bodega, and so this unlikely foursome leaves the Ugly Dog and starts walking south on Avenue B.

"What do you guys do?" asks Val. She likes Tom and Dave. It's cool hanging out with guys who can buy beer no problem.

"We're roadies for a band," says Tom.

"That's so cool," says Val. "What band?"

"Lots of bands, but lately for Roadkill, a punk band. Have you heard of them?" asks Tom.

"Sorry, no," says Val.

"Roadies for Roadkill," says Stephie bitterly.

"Shut up," whispers Val.

"What do you guys do?" asks Tom. "You look like you're freshmen in college."

"We're in—" but before Stephie can say, "We're in high

school," Val cuts her off and says, "Yeah, we're freshmen at Hofstra, in Long Island."

"Cool," says Tom. "I did two years at William Paterson College, but then I dropped out. I'd like to go back someday." Tom is quiet a moment, thinking how it would be good to get a degree, and then he says, "Listen, before we get more beer we need to pick up this package for our friend Tony. He's a good guy, he gets a lot of work for us. We just have to stop at this guy's place on Fourth Street to pick it up."

"Yeah, Tony is really cool," says Dave.

"Okay," says Val. "That's fine with me."

Stephie wants to cry. How much more can she take? She doesn't like the sound of a package, but she tags along anyway, sticking with Val. And as they walk down the street, her wet foot is freezing. She'd love to complain about it, but she's too embarrassed to tell Val what happened in the bathroom. Her toes ache. *I'm going to get frostbite from stepping in a toilet.*

They turn down Fourth Street and they come to an abandoned building.

"We'll be right back. You guys wait here," says Tom, indicating the doorway.

"Do people live here?" asks Val.

"Yeah, it's a squat, but it's a good one," says Tom. "They have electricity and everything."

"I live in a squat," says Dave to impress Val and Stephie, and then the two guys go in the building.

"I can't believe we're doing this," says Stephie.

"I know! It's so cool."

"Do you have any idea how stupid this is?"

"Look, they get this package and then we all go get some

beers. What's the big deal? It's New Year's Eve, for Christ's sake."

"But we don't even know these guys! We don't even know what's in that package," Stephie says, and then she whispers, even though they're all alone, "Val, it could be *heroin* for all we know." Heroin seems, to Stephie, like the kind of word that should be whispered.

"You know," says Val, "you're really starting to bring me down with this pessimistic bullshit."

"Pessimistic? We're probably going to get arrested for being drug runners!"

"That's better than being a runner on the track team," says Val, who really is more bark than bite. She's quite rebellious, but if she actually did get arrested she'd be crying just as hard as Stephie.

Before the two girls can argue further, Tom and Dave emerge from the tenement. Dave is carrying a foot-long, paper-wrapped rectangular package.

"So we'll get some beer, but then we gotta go back to the club," says Tom, "and bring the package to Tony."

"Sure, that's cool," says Val.

Stephie stares at the package with fear. She doesn't like to be near it. "So . . . what's in the package?" she manages to ask.

"It's . . . like I said, it's for Tony," says Tom. He looks away from the girls, he's evasive.

"For Tony," says Stephie. "This is too crazy . . . I'm not getting arrested. I'm going home."

Stephie starts off toward B, and away from the heroin, which is sometimes known as H. For Stephie, New York gets worse as you climb the alphabet.

Val runs after her. Tom and Dave wait at the tenement, perplexed. "Where you going?" asks Val.

"To the train station! I'm getting out of here before these jerks get us killed."

"You wanted to hang out with a band—these guys are musicians."

"They're roadies, Val. For Roadkill. There's a huge difference between roadies and guys in a band."

Stephie again starts off. She's going home. She's had enough. Her foot is freezing.

Val follows after her. She has a confession to make. "Look, Stephie," she says, "I didn't tell you something because I knew you'd spaz out. But the last train left an hour ago."

Stephie stops walking; she's on B. The Avenue of Rape. "Are you telling me we're stranded here for the night?"

Tom and Dave approach. "Hey, sorry," Tom says, "but Tony is expecting us. We gotta get back to the club. So, you guys coming?"

"Yeah, we're coming," says Val, knowing that Stephie doesn't really have a choice. And Val's glad. Because she needs Stephie along. Stephie's a drag, but she helps keep things a little normal. And by Stephie carrying around most of the worries and fears, Val doesn't have to worry. She's free to have a good time, while Stephie is miserable. Friendships are often symbiotic that way, and Val intuitively and subconsciously senses this.

And Tom is glad that the two girls are coming along. Well, he's glad that Val is coming. He likes her. "We're all set, then," Tom says. "Let's get some beers."

"Bevo," says Dave, and then he says, acting important, "I

got the package." He says this to try to score points with Stephie (he knows that Tom wants Val, so he gets the second-best girl, that's how it works), but like his bragging about living in a squat, Stephie is not charmed.

25

Eric and Monica are sitting on her couch, which is flush against the wall. Eric has a refilled wineglass. *Love Story* has been shut off so that no more wine will be thrown, and Bing Crosby has been taken off the record player. The Go-Go's have replaced old B. C. and his Christmas crooning. Eric is opening up to Monica, and Monica is listening, partly out of sympathy, and partly because she doesn't want him to leave. Also, she doesn't mind his complaining as long as he's not destroying her dips.

"I mean, what's so wrong with me, anyway?" Eric whines. "I'm a nice guy, right? I'm successful . . . I'm not bad to look at . . . But for some reason, every woman I go out with breaks up with me! Why is that, Monica?"

Oh, God, I don't like where this is going. She tries to avoid

Eric's question as best she can. "Oh, well, I don't know. Lots of reasons, probably," she says lightly, offhandedly.

"Right, it's always lots of reasons! I've never once gotten a straight answer out of any of you! Like you—what was your reason?"

"Eric, really . . . who remembers?"

"You don't remember?!? It was only six months ago." For Eric, this breakup with Monica is now recent history. But earlier in the night, in his argument with Bridget, it was ancient history. This is one of the fascinating things about time. It's like an accordion—it is continually expanding and collapsing, all depending on the human perspective of the moment, because it is humans who have invented time.

"Well, six months is a long time," says Monica, expanding the accordion.

"Six months is nothing!" shouts Eric, collapsing the accordion, but getting ready to burst again like an aneurysm.

"Will you calm down? Jesus."

"Okay, fine—you can't remember the lame excuse you gave me six months ago for breaking up with me? I'll tell you! The reason was: You liked me as a friend, but not as a boyfriend, even though you found me attractive!"

"That's not lame," says Monica. *That's a damn good breakup line; one of the best I ever came up with.*

"It makes no sense whatsoever!" Eric is ready to go varicose again. He can hardly take what's happening to him. *These women are driving me insane.*

"Well, I think it makes sense."

"See, that's what I'm talking about! That's what I'm dealing with—these crazy leaps of reasoning. And they sound logical at first, but later, when you think about it, they don't make any sense at all. You were attracted to me but you didn't want me to be your boyfriend. Where's the logic in that?"

"Eric, you have got to calm down."

"I mean, all I want is the truth, you know? If you're breaking up with me, tell me why. Is that too much to ask? . . . But wait a second. Let's just forget it. I give up! I'm through with all of you." Eric thinks of throwing his wineglass at the TV again, but the blank screen isn't as provoking as Ryan O'Neal's face. So instead of throwing his wine, Eric drains it, gets up, grabs his coat, and heads for Monica's door.

Monica races after him. "Wait. What are you doing?"

"I'm going home," Eric says, stopping at the door.

"Home! But you just got here," she says desperately, and then she throws her body against the door for the second time this night, for the second time in her life. With beseeching eyes, she looks at Eric, who is stunned by this cinematic maneuver, this throwing of one's body against a door. He has never seen it before either, except in movies. "Eric, please," she says, "I'm begging you—don't do this! Don't leave me. Don't go!" Monica hardly recognizes the words coming out of her mouth. She feels like she's in a movie, something like *Wuthering Heights*. Her desperation has left her without her own words. Like throwing her body against the door, she has to borrow lines from old black-and-white films.

Eric, seeing her utter vulnerability, offers a deal. But perhaps it's a bargain with the Devil. It's an old maxim, but a good one—be careful of asking for what you want. "Okay, fine," he says. "You want me to stay? Then tell me the truth!"

"What?!?"

"Tell me why you broke up with me—the real reason—and I'll stay."

Monica hesitates. The Devil is now tempting her. He is playing with both these young people. The Devil always finds his way in when you think you really desire and need something. Perhaps the way to heaven or heaven here on earth is to realize you want for nothing. But Eric wants the truth, and Monica wants a guest. But Monica hesitates to give Eric what he wants. So Eric grabs the doorknob, he will attempt to swing the door open with Monica pressed against it. She knows that this is possible, since Hillary has already done so. "Okay, I'll tell you," she blurts out. "Oh God . . ."

"Let's hear it," Eric says, letting go of the doorknob.

"Well, I can't speak for why Bridget broke up with you tonight, or any of the others . . . but for me . . ." She stops. Can she really do this? *Who ever tells another person the truth about a breakup? It's never been done before.* But she has to go for it. She needs a goddamn guest. "The truth is," she says, "I broke up with you because you were the worst lover I ever had in my life."

Eric was expecting something bad. Something about his character. Perhaps that he was self-centered. But this? Bad in bed? "What?" he manages to say. Perhaps he heard wrong.

"I'm serious," says Monica, perhaps going too far with this truth-telling. "It was bad. Even counting high school, and the guys in high school were really bad."

Eric hangs his head and looks down at his crotch. He feels like he has the smallest penis in the world.

26

Back in the Kiev, in the ladies' bathroom, Kevin's average-sized penis is pressing against Lucy's rear end. After some discussion, Lucy and Kevin have opted to do it doggie-style. Lucy, they figure, should bend over the toilet, her hands on the back of the porcelain, and Kevin will mount her that way. He will be close to the door, but they figure there will be just enough room. Right now they're warming up with some standing-up spooning: Kevin behind Lucy, rubbing, as mentioned, his penis against her ass. They still have all their clothes on. They are enjoying themselves, though they do feel a little awkward, a little mechanical. But overall, they are having a good time, despite, as Kevin predicted, the putrid smell of air freshener.

Kevin puts his face in Lucy's hair and escalates the eroticism of their spooning by reaching around and gently fondling Lucy's breasts. They feel good to him, which catches him off guard. *I'm on second with Lucy. My friend Lucy. I can't believe my friend has boobs. You're friends with a girl and you forget she has all these great things—like breasts.*

Lucy, meanwhile, likes the pressure of Kevin's penis against her rear. *He's really hard, I love it when a guy's really hard.*

They decided on doggie-style for practical reasons. A man and woman can almost never successfully have intercourse while standing face-to-face. It's been done, but rarely. In the movies, the man will often lift a woman up against a wall and enter her forcefully while she happily wraps her legs around his back. But this is more of Hollywood's bullshit. This position has been done, of course—intercourse has occurred at every conceivable angle—but not with the unrealistic frequency displayed on the silver screen. It's hard enough for a man to get a hard-on, but then for him to lift a woman and to then thrust like an Olympian, achieving his-and-her simultaneous climaxes in thirty-five seconds, is pure Tinseltown mythmaking.

Also, Kevin and Lucy have opted for doggie-style because they really don't want to see each other's faces. After all, they have known each other for five years and to have to expose to one another their lovemaking face, like a game-day face in professional sports, is asking too much of this New Year's Eve bathroom copulation between friends.

So then Kevin decides it's time to unzip Lucy's black miniskirt. He could just lift up the skirt and pull the panties down, but he thinks that's too anonymous. But the zipper is jammed. He kneels down to study it.

"What are you doing?" asks Lucy.

"Trying to get this zipper down."

"Is it stuck?"

"Yeah."

"I'll do it," she says, and she reaches behind herself and yanks down on the unmovable zipper. But because the zipper doesn't move, her elbow flares out and goes right into Kevin's eye. Unfortunately, he is still squatting at ass level.

"Oh, Jesus!" he bellows in agony.

"Sorry," says Lucy.

"I can't see! I'm blinded."

He stands up, rubbing his eye. Lucy yanks on the zipper and it rips. "I didn't like this skirt, anyway," she says, and she lets it fall to her ankles. She's now only wearing her black tights (no panties, it seems), and she turns, with skirt-shackled ankles, to inspect the injured Kevin. He squints at her. "Your eye all right?" she asks.

"Yeah," he says. "I may never paint again, now that I'm half blind, but my paintings suck anyway."

"Let's take your shirt off," she says, wanting to keep the focus on sex and away from Kevin's lousy art career.

"Okay," he says.

She begins to help Kevin lift up his tight black turtleneck. But because of the confines of the bathroom stall, and the turtleneck's tightness, they struggle and the turtleneck gets stuck around Kevin's head.

"Now I really can't see . . . This whole thing is ridiculous."

"I know," says Lucy. "But we've come this far." She pulls some more on the turtleneck.

"That's my nose!"

"I've almost got it over your head." She yanks hard, as she did on the zipper, but the turtleneck doesn't give, an annoying feature of this type of garment, and the force of her failed effort sends her tumbling backward, where she lands hard on the toilet seat, but not in the toilet, which is something to be grateful for.

Kevin is still blinded, but his hearing, made more acute by his blindness, lets him know that Lucy has fallen. "Are you all right?" he asks.

"Oh, I'm just *great*," she says, but with the fierce resiliency of the female sex she takes a breath, stands up, grabs hold of that turtleneck, and with one massive heave removes it, revealing a smiling, liberated Kevin. The turtleneck falls to the grimy floor, and the two friends after all this struggle are face to face, looking into each other's eyes. Like musicians playing together and knowing intuitively what to do next, Lucy and Kevin are in that sudden perfect place of harmony that sometimes happens between a man and a woman.

So they kiss.

And it's a good kiss.

Tender. Satisfying. Passionate. Hot. Chemical. Charged. Tasty. Makes you want more. A good fit. Just the right amount of saliva. No dry lips. And also present in the kiss is the thing that no one has been able to put an exact finger on—the yin and yang of it, the positive and negative, the north and south, the east and west, the army and navy . . . man and woman.

Then they part. A little embarrassed. It's like they've received a surprise inheritance and they feel funny about being nouveau riche.

But also, Lucy's heart has been touched. So has Kevin's.

"I mean, we're just having some fun, right?" she asks, flustered.

"Right," says Kevin, also flustered.

But to hell with fluster. They go to kiss again, but then the bathroom door opens, so they don't kiss. They are not alone. A quite attractive young woman, a dark, stylish brunette, has come in to pee. Kevin and Lucy, like children playing hide-and-go-seek, hold their breath. And the anxiety of playing hide-and-go-seek makes *them* want to pee. And, ironically, they are in a toilet but they can't use it. The attractive young woman approaches the stall, the only one, and naturally she looks to the floor to see if there are any shoes—the universal indicator that someone is on the can. To the young lady's surprise, she sees two pairs of shoes, a man's and woman's.

"Kevin?" says the young woman, and Kevin knows the voice but doesn't say anything. Now he really has to pee. "You think I don't recognize the shoes?" she asks, and then she shouts, "I bought them for you, you bastard, remember?"

"Ellie—" Kevin says, pleading, and he bends down to pick up his turtleneck off the floor and on the way up, his shoulder accidentally releases the toilet door's latch and the door swings open. Ellie stares at her half-naked, just-broken-up-with ex-boyfriend.

Kevin presses his turtleneck against his male bosom, trying to cover up, and Lucy just stands there, in her black tights, her skirt at her ankles. Ellie takes this all in.

"I should've known!" Ellie says.

"What are you doing here?" asks Kevin, unable to come up with anything better.

"I had to go to the bathroom. That's what normal people do in here."

"Wow, this is really an incredible coincidence," says Kevin, trying to make this a funny, comic moment, and then he looks to Lucy, who is pulling up her skirt, and asks, "Isn't this an incredible coincidence?"

"Incredible," says Lucy, holding up her miniskirt.

"You were just so brokenhearted, weren't you? You couldn't even wait twenty-four hours to throw yourself at her."

"But she's just a friend," says Kevin. "You remember Lucy."

Lucy smiles at Ellie and reaches behind herself and buttons the skirt, but the zipper is shot.

"Did you have to bring her here?" asks Ellie. "The Kiev is *our* place." She turns to leave this sordid scene.

Kevin steps out of the stall. "Ellie, wait! Where are you going?"

She faces her horrible ex-boyfriend. "To call my therapist!"

"You can't reach your therapist on New Year's Eve!"

"I happen to be staying at his place."

Kevin is now completely out of the stall, so Lucy closes the door and sits on the toilet, fishes a cigarette out of her purse, and lights up.

"That's unprofessional, it might even be illegal," says Kevin. "You're not supposed to shack up with your therapist. And what's he think about you taking an ax to Freud's head?"

"Don't bring my work into this, and I'm not shacking up with him. It's just until I get a place of my own. Remember I used to live with you . . . *yesterday!*"

Ellie opens the bathroom door and she begins to cry. Kevin doesn't see her tears and says, "What's the matter? You went to your therapist because there wasn't any room at Jack's?"

She turns and looks at him; she's confused. "Jack's?"

"That's right! I heard all about it—the whole story. How you were sleeping with him the whole time we were together."

"I never slept with Jack!"

Lucy makes sure that the stall door is locked. She takes several quick, nervous hits off her cigarette.

"What?" says Kevin.

"You're insane . . . and I had really thought I was wrong about you, Kevin. I tried calling you tonight, to ask *you* to take *me* back. But you weren't in. So I was going to try again tomorrow. I wanted to move back in—isn't that pathetic?" Now a real flood of tears comes out and she sobs and runs out of the bathroom.

Kevin, still holding his turtleneck to his torso, doesn't try to chase after her, he merely calls out, hopelessly, "Ellie . . ."

Lucy, from the safety of her locked stall, says, "Okay. So I was wrong about Jack."

"She never slept with him," he says quietly, almost to himself.

"I was just telling you what I heard."

"She was coming back to me. She tried to call. If I had been home, where I should have been, everything would be all right. It was just a twenty-four-hour breakup . . . now it's permanent."

"Look, I'm sorry," says Lucy.

Kevin goes to the sink and splashes water on his face. For the first time all night, he feels quite sober.

"Kevin? . . . Do you forgive me?" she asks. But he doesn't

say anything. He just continues to bathe his face. Lucy stays on the toilet, smoking, and she wants to ask him, "What about *our* kiss?" But she doesn't ask. Instead she pulls down her tights and pees. And peeing makes her think of all the drinks she had at that bar, and then she thinks of the *bartender*. All is not lost.

27

Bridget and Caitlyn have just finished making plans to go with the quarterback-bartender (let's call him QB for short) to his party, which they still don't realize is Eric's ex-girlfriend's party. QB begins to close out his register. He's getting midnight off because he worked Christmas Eve and Christmas Day (Jack Dempsey's, naturally, was open; it's an Irish bar).

While QB squares away his money, Bridget and Caitlyn decide to wait outside for him. Bridget didn't think it would look good, to whomever would be looking, to be seen going off with a bartender, even though she's quite happy with the idea. He's much better looking than Eric, and has to be better in bed.

Out on Second Avenue, Bridget rubs her hands together to try and stay warm. "It's freezing, isn't it?" she says.

"What are you complaining about?" says Caitlyn. "You're the one who's so desperate to wait for this bartender."

"What's your problem?" asks Bridget, not liking Caitlyn's catty tone.

"I don't have a problem," says Caitlyn.

"All right, good, I'm glad."

"Still, I just can't believe we're freezing to death so you can throw yourself at some bartender when it's after ten on New Year's Eve and neither of us has a date."

"You know what I think?" says Bridget. "I think you're jealous because he picked me!"

"Excuse me—"

"That's right! You can't stand that any guy would pick me over you! You just don't want me to have a boyfriend."

"That's bullshit. What about Jonathan? I was really glad when you two started going out!"

"Jonathan is your brother!"

"So?"

"The point is, you can't stand that the bartender chose me! It's just eating away at you because you're always so competitive about guys!"

"I am not competitive! And anyway, he didn't 'choose' you!"

"Who do you think he was inviting to this party?"

"As I recall," says Caitlyn, "he invited us both."

"No he didn't. He only had to include you to be polite. But he was looking at me the whole time!"

"You are living in a dream world!"

Bridget takes a step toward Caitlyn. Bridget's nostrils flare. *I might have to slap this slut-bitch.*

Caitlyn notices the dilation of Bridget's nostrils. *I think this bitch-slut is going to slap me.*

"I'm warning you, Caitlyn," says Bridget. "Keep your slutty hands off my bartender."

"He isn't *your* bartender! He's *our* bartender!"

"Listen, you talked me into breaking up with Eric. You owe me this bartender! He's a hunk and he wants *me*, not you. Me!"

"Oh, you think so?" asks Caitlyn. *I might have to slap this bitch-slut.*

"Yeah, I do think so," says Bridget. *I might have to slap this slut-bitch.*

The two face off. New Year's Eve traffic flows by on Second Avenue. People, huddled in their winter coats, are walking quickly to parties (though not to Monica's party). But Bridget and Caitlyn are oblivious to New York City, to the world. Only one thing could break their concentration and their female rage against one another. The object of their desires. The man.

So QB steps outside and the battle of the same-sexes comes to an immediate halt. "So it's still kind of early for a party," says the unsuspecting QB. "What do you girls say we go get a drink? It always relaxes me after work to have somebody pour *me* a drink."

Bridget and Caitlyn respond in exactly the same way to QB—they give him their most alluring, come-hither, flirtatious smiles and they both say, "Sure. A drink. I'd love to." Then they both look at one another, with hate, but they are linked verbally in some odd way and so then they both say at the same time, "We'd love to."

"Jinx," says QB, playing the old kids' game. "Now you both can't talk."

The girls give fake laughs. Nothing is going to stop these two from talking. QB flags down a taxi and tells the driver to go to Fourteenth Street. They all slide in the back seat, with QB in the middle. The taxi pulls off, and Bridget and Caitlyn, still in a strange competitive duet, in which they say and do the same exact thing, each put a hand on one of QB's knees. He smiles happily. Bridget strokes his left knee, Caitlyn his right. Who will get to sack the quarterback?

28

Jack waits at the table in Gandhi II and sips his wine. Cindy is in the bathroom weeping, feeling sorry for herself. She's lost her virginity and as a result has become the world's greatest klutz, as if her hymen had controlled some kind of mechanism of balance. In one night she has broken up an Irish bar and an Indian restaurant. She is overwhelmed with shame and confusion.

As Jack waits for Cindy, he notices that all the other patrons in the restaurant are women. They've all come here on same-sex dates because they couldn't get men on New Year's Eve. He feels like he's in a cafeteria at Smith College, albeit one with twinkling Christmas lights and sitar music, and all these lonely women give him an uncomfortable feeling.

Then the waiter leads two young women past Jack's table.

One of the women stops and says, "Jack?" The waiter takes the other woman to the empty table.

Jack looks up at the woman beside him. She's a chubby blonde with a cute face. He can't remember her name. He does remember that he had a one-night stand with her about five weeks ago, and that they had spoken once or twice afterward. Then he stopped calling her. And now his brain is seizing up. It's the dreaded Ex-Lover Name Lock.

"Oh, hi," he says weakly.

"I'm Cheryl," she spits out, seeing in his face that she's on the receiving end of the humiliating Ex-Lover Name Lock. "I can't believe you don't even remember my name."

"What are you talking about, Cheryl? I know your name . . . So how are you doing? Happy New Year."

"You said you were going out of town for New Year's."

Jack remembers that she had tried to pin him down for New Year's Eve. More than a month in advance! He never makes plans that far ahead. He doesn't make plans two days ahead. Too much pressure. Also, he knew after the first night that he didn't want to pursue things with Cheryl. When he picked her up in the bar, she was wearing a thick sweater. She had hidden her chubbiness, which he discovered only when they were in bed. And Jack is very particular when it comes to women. Like many American men, he was raised on *Playboy* magazine and so he holds women to a very difficult, airbrushed standard.

And now Jack can't remember the excuse he gave her for New Year's Eve. Not only has the sudden appearance of this girl caused Name Lock, but it has also caused Lie Lock. "Did I say I was going out of town for New Year's Eve? You got it wrong. I was away for Christmas."

"You said you'd be gone all week."

"Oh, that's right. I was going on this ski trip, but it got canceled right after you and I talked. So I was going to be out of town, but it was so long ago, what with the holidays, that I forgot I was ever going to go on that trip."

"You said you were flying to L.A. to audition for a sitcom."

"That's why I didn't go on the ski trip. But then the audition was canceled."

Cheryl is incredulous at the stream of lies coming out of this man's mouth. And she's hurt and pissed off and humiliated that they had sex and that he has forgotten her name.

"I can't believe I was stupid enough to go home with you," she says. "I actually thought I liked you."

"Cheryl—"

"Just do me a favor. Don't call me again, okay?" she says, trying to salvage her pride, not that Jack would call her again.

So then Cheryl angrily walks off and joins her friend at their table. She sits down and immediately points at Jack and says something to her companion. Jack turns around to make an attempt at a conciliatory remark to Cheryl, but he sees how she's pointing at him and so he feebly smiles, a smile that's meant to convey apology, but Cheryl gives him the finger.

He turns back around and looks at all the lonely women. It's a small restaurant, only a dozen tables, but it strikes him that it's quite strange and bizarre that he's the only male—besides the waiters—in the whole restaurant. Granted, there are more women than men in New York, and more single women than any city in the U.S., but still it's a demographic freak of nature that Jack is so outnumbered, and he senses intuitively that he's in hostile, enemy territory. This strange

harem of single women is all staring at him. They eaves-
dropped on his conversation with Cheryl and they've judged
him for what he is—a cad. And the worst kind: a good-looking
cad.

Jack perceives this mob hatred, throws a twenty down on
the table, grabs his coat and Cindy's coat, and heads for the
ladies' room. He's going to get his deflowered date and get the
hell out of Gandhi II. He doesn't like the vibe in the whole
place, and also he's afraid that when Cindy comes back to the
table Cheryl might say something. So this is a preemptive
retreat out of danger. He must protect his troops. Actually, his
troop. His one soldier—himself.

He knocks at the ladies' room door. "Cindy? You okay in
there?"

Cindy is sitting on the toilet, quietly sobbing. Jack's knock
and voice startle her. "I'm fine, I'm fine," she says with a mild
tone of hysteria, but Jack can't perceive this through the bathroom door. It muffles hysteria.

"So are you about ready to leave, then? Because I'd really
like to get out of here, you know?"

"Almost," says Cindy, and she gets up off the toilet and goes
to the sink and splashes cold water on her face, trying to
reduce the swelling in her eyes from the crying. Jack puts his
ear to the bathroom door to hear what she's doing, he wants
her to hurry up already, and then the bald waiter comes and
stares at Jack. He doesn't like the tip that Jack has left. The bill
was eighteen dollars and Jack left twenty. Not even fifteen per-
cent and the girl made a mess. And now this boy has his ear
against the ladies' room.

"Please don't stand there like that," says the waiter in his

British colonial accent, taking the moral upper hand. "It's not proper."

Jack steps away from the bathroom door and the bald, overworked waiter continues on to the kitchen. Jack steps back to the door and says, "We're making a scene out here. Will you please hurry up?"

Cindy opens the door a crack, and peeks out at Jack. She's wretched. Her eyes are puffy, her hair has collapsed and hangs around her face like wet leaves, and her cocktail dress is all smeared and wet.

"Are you all right?" asks Jack. "You look like you're going to throw up."

This provokes a new rush of tears on Cindy's part. When it comes to releasing water, men are great sweaters, women are great criers.

Snot begins to pour out of Cindy's nose—the unfortunate result of crying is a buildup of mucus in the nasal passages. Cindy wipes her nose with the back of her hand.

Jack is at a loss as to how to comfort this girl. He wonders if all virgins are this insane the day after. "So you ate a chili, so what? It's no big deal," he says. "Let's just get out of here. Get some fresh air."

"Sure, you say that now," she says, the tears abating somewhat. "But tomorrow it will be another story. Tomorrow it'll be—'Oh, no, there's that chili girl calling again!'"

Jack wonders if she's psychic. That will probably be his exact response, with perhaps a few other modifiers, like the virgin-chandelier-smasher chili girl.

"I'm not going to think of you as the chili girl," he says. "But let's leave and talk about this outside."

"I just wanted everything to be perfect, you know," says Cindy, still standing in the crack of the ladies' room door. "Because I really think you're the most . . ." But Cindy stops. She's too embarrassed to say it. But she's got Jack again; this hint of forthcoming praise has him feeling tenderly toward her. She's His Wonderful Virgin Girl again.

"I'm the most what? What?"

Cindy comes up with an alternative. "I really think you're a very nice person, Jack."

This is disappointing to our young, ego-hungry actor. "You think I'm *nice?*"

"You are," says Cindy. "Remember last night at the bar, when I got that nosebleed?" Cindy's nose, dry from the cold December air, had bled at the bar last night, unexpectedly. Now that she thinks of it, that nosebleed was an odd omen of what was to come. But Jack had been so sweet about her nosebleed, offering her a napkin and telling her to squeeze the top of her nose to stop the bleeding. "A lot of guys wouldn't look at a girl after she has a nosebleed. But you were so nice about it."

Before Jack can reply to this odd nosebleed compliment, he senses something behind him. He looks back and sees Cheryl with her friend and two other women from an adjoining table pointing at him and talking about him.

"Come on, let's take this outside, we'll go to the party."

"What? Okay," she says and steps out of the bathroom and makes to return to the table. She sees four women approaching the bathroom, but doesn't think anything of it.

Jack grabs her arm and says, "I already paid, and here's your coat. Let's go out the back way."

He quickly leads her through the kitchen, past the scowling

waiter, who is taking a break, having a cup of tea, and out the back exit into the alleyway behind Sixth Street.

Jack leads Cindy down the alleyway and the waiter pokes his head out the back door and shouts, "You're a bad tipper and a bad man! Stay away from ladies' rooms. I never want to see you here again!"

Cindy looks at Jack and giggles. And he smiles at her. They're in an alleyway that smells terribly of rotting food and Jack is being yelled at by a waiter, but it's their best moment all night. She doesn't know why, really, that they're rushing out of the restaurant, but it feels like it's an escape and it's fun. Jack knows why they're fleeing, but it's fun for him too, in a way. It's daring, and for both of them it's romantic. They feel sort of Bonnie and Clydish.

29

Eric is pouring himself a gin and tonic, mostly gin. He's been dealt one of the greatest blows a man can receive—he's been told he's lousy in bed. Almost nothing else will hurt a man quite like that. He can lose money, he can lose his hair, he can lose his favorite dog, but tell him he's a loser in bed and you'll break his will to live.

So Eric takes a big gulp of his drink and then angrily and sexually thrusts a cracker into the crab dip. Some of the crab dip falls onto the table before it can reach his mouth. Every time he goes near the table, he makes a mess of it.

Monica is standing by her window, looking down to the street for a guest. It's ten-thirty and she has only one person at her party—a sexually handicapped ex-boyfriend.

Eric takes another gulp of his drink and then addresses

Monica: "I'm okay sizewise, right? My dimensions, I think, are well within the standard range of human proportions. I've been in locker rooms." *Then again, everybody's flaccid in locker rooms. I'm going to measure myself as soon as I go home . . . As long as I'm at least six inches I'm normal. Please, God, let me be six inches. Do I measure from the bottom or the top? Would a doctor know?*

"It isn't your dimensions," says Monica impatiently. "That's not your problem."

This is mildly reassuring to Eric, but he still plans to take out the tape measure when he gets home. He thinks of other faults he might possess. "Well, I know there was the time I fell asleep," he says, "but I was tired. I'm only human!"

"Eric, it wasn't that either."

"Well, then, what was it? What was so horrible that you never even gave me a chance, Monica? A person can make progress, you know . . . learn new techniques. There are lots of books I could read."

"No, I don't think that would help."

"So, in your opinion, I'm hopeless? Are you saying—flat out—that I should just give up sex?"

"Well, you still have your work. Your gallery loves you."

"My work! Who gives a shit?" He starts jabbing crackers into all the dips, making havoc, eating the crackers, and making crumbs. Compulsive eating, they say, like chewing ice, is a way to express sexual frustration. Eric waves a crab-dipped cracker in the air and says, "So my art career is good, but I stink at sex. Thanks for telling me that, Monica, that's a great comfort . . . But don't you fucking realize that the whole point of having a career, of any kind, is to get women in bed? So what good is being successful if I'm a lousy lover?"

Monica comes back over to the table, to try and fix it *again*. Eric is driving her nuts. If any guests ever do show up—and she's not without some hope, because people keep hoping almost as long as they're breathing—she would like her buffet table to be attractive. But Eric keeps wrecking it. She brushes some crumbs into a napkin and says to Eric, "Look, some things just can't be helped. You have to accept your limitations."

"Can't be helped? This has to be the worst night of my life. You invite me over here and I come because I feel sorry for you, because you tell me you're scared nobody will come. So I come, even though I've been broken up with, and then you repay me by telling me I'm the worst lover you've ever had and that there's nothing I can do about it."

He shoves a cracker so violently into the poor assaulted crab dip that some of the crab dip flies out and lands against the side of a bottle of red wine. They both watch the dip slide down the bottle.

Monica can't take any more. The sliding crab dip pushes her over the edge. "Look, Eric, I'm sorry Bridget dumped you!" she exclaims, but then she begins to cry. Eric is confused by this. "And I'm sorry you're bad in bed," she continues through her tears, "but more than anything I'm sorry I decided to throw this atrocity—this nightmarish ordeal of a New Year's party, because it is breaking me. You understand? This party is breaking me!"

She lets loose a wail, which sounds like a cough, and then she throws herself against Eric and cries and snots on his shirt. He puts his hands tentatively on her shoulders.

"Monica, come on," he says, making an effort to comfort her, "it's not that bad. *I'm* here."

"Not that bad?" More tears flow. "We've got a hostess who's crying and one guest who's coming to terms with his sexual inadequacy. That's it! That's my party! Not even my desperate teenage cousin from Long Island came to my party. Well, happy fucking New Year!"

Eric wraps his arms around her completely now. "Monica," he says sweetly, soothingly, and he rubs her back. She cries and wails and moans and presses against him. Eric keeps rubbing her back and he feels himself getting a hard-on. He wonders if it's bad form to get a hard-on while she's crying. He thinks of pulling back his hips. But he decides to leave the hard-on there. *Let her feel it. It's huge. It's got to be more than six inches. I hope she can feel it . . . Maybe she'll let me have sex with her and I can redeem myself.*

Monica, unaware of Eric's hard-on, continues to cry.

30

Tom, Dave, Val, and Stephie, after picking up a six-pack at the bodega, return to the smoke-filled Ugly Dog on Avenue B. The music has been raised to even more deafening levels. Legions of young punk rockers will be wearing hearing aids when they hit their forties and fifties.

Our foursome finds some chairs in the corner and makes this their base. It happens to be near the bathrooms. Stephie glances fearfully at the door to the horrible ladies' room, where her foot was plunged into the toilet bowl.

Stephie shouts to Val over the music: "I've got to be crazy letting you drag me back to this snake pit!"

Then Tom shouts to Val: "We gotta go find Tony! You guys stay here. We'll be right back."

"Cool!" shouts Val.

Then Tom leans in, *You gotta show a girl you like her,* and gives Val a kiss. Val really responds, and the kiss, which had started out as a sweet peck, becomes a passionate French kiss, with Val as the aggressor. Dave watches Tom and Val with a big smile on his double-chinned face. And Stephie looks on with horror, sees Val's tongue for an instant before it disappears in Tom's mouth, and she thinks to look away, but she can't.

Then Val and Tom break apart. Tom smiles, and then he and Dave head to the bar to deliver the package, which Dave has under his arm.

"I can't believe you Frenched him," says Stephie.

"Will you grow up already . . . I gotta go pee. Wait for me here."

"Don't go in there, that toilet's gross," says Stephie.

"I gotta go," says Val, and she leaves Stephie, who looks down at her boot. *At least it's starting to dry.*

Stephie is left all alone with the six-pack. She opens one, takes a sip, and lights a cigarette. She looks around. The bar reminds her of the bar in *Star Wars.* She wishes she had a Han Solo with her, or an Obi-Wan Kenobi. Somebody to protect her. Then she thinks of Val in the toilet. *I hope she falls in like I did.*

Val comes back. Stephie looks at Val's boots—they're both dry. *Damn, nothing bad ever happens to her.*

Tom and Dave come back, too, and Dave still has the package.

"I thought you were supposed to be giving that to your friend," says Stephie.

"He's not here," says Tom. "He went to this party on Avenue D—we'll have to find him there."

"What?" says Stephie, going pale beneath her rouge, her sparkly eye glitter losing its sparkle.

"Cool," says Val, and Tom and Dave sit down, and everybody has a beer.

"Did you say Avenue D?" asks Stephie. "D like dog? Like death?"

"Yeah," says Tom, and then he lifts his beer and says, "Happy New Year," and they all clink bottles, even Stephie. Dave chugs his whole beer, and then opens another and downs half of that.

Tom finishes off his bottle, grabs another, and then says to Val, "You wanna dance?"

"Yeah!" says Val, and they go to the dance floor with their beers, leaving Stephie with Dave.

Dave chugs down his second beer—he doesn't have that belly for nothing—and then he asks Val, "Could I have a sip of your beer?"

Stephie hands him her beer and he starts chugging that one. And she's relieved, she didn't want to drink from it after his lips were on it. Then he puts the empty beer on the floor, puts the package on Tom's seat, and then he puts his big meaty arm around Stephie. He leans in for a kiss. It's what Tom told him to do. And he saw it work with Val.

Stephie doesn't scream, but her natural reaction is to turn away in horror. She swivels her head completely to the left and almost into the face of a punk-rock girl who has green spikes coming out of her head. The girl doesn't like Stephie crowding her like that, so she sticks out her tongue, which she somehow has managed to dye black.

Stephie sees this fat black snake of tongue, Dave gets her

ear in his mouth, having missed her lips, and now she screams—a guttural yelp—and she is able to slither out of Dave's arms.

She staggers to the dance floor to get Val and then get out of the Ugly Dog once and for all. She doesn't care—she'll sleep in Penn Station and get the first morning train to Ronkonkoma. So she wades into the writhing, slam-dancing hordes, but she can't spot Val. She goes all the way into the middle and finds herself trapped there by a wall of bodies. She struggles for a moment, trying to push her way out, but she is repelled back into the center. Something in her snaps, gives up, but in a good way. As Napoleon said, "When rape is imminent, sit back and enjoy it." So Stephie begins to dance with the ghoulish punkers. She closes her eyes and she loses herself and she slams around and writhes with the best of them.

31

Kevin pays the cashier at the Kiev and storms out of the restaurant, heading up Second Avenue. Lucy is trailing after him.

"Will you please wait up?" she says.

He doesn't slow down, but Lucy, stepping up her pace, manages to walk beside him.

"How could I have been so stupid?" he says. "Of course Ellie would show up. Given that it was the worst possible thing that could happen, it should've been obvious! It's your fault, Lucy."

They come to the intersection of Second and St. Marks Place. The street is abuzz with New Year's Eve. They stop at the crosswalk. The don't walk sign is flashing. They obey this red neon command.

"So it's *my* fault," Lucy says, "that your girlfriend caught you dry humping in a bathroom stall?"

"Do you have to be so crude? I've always hated that about you."

"I wasn't hearing any complaints when you had your hands on my tits."

A fat fifty-year-old man, who has just bought several dirty magazines for his New Year's celebration (he usually only buys one a week, but tonight he splurged and bought three), walks past Kevin and Lucy and hears the word "tits" and his ears perk up. He looks at Lucy and smiles. She's made his night.

"You think this is a big joke, don't you?" says Kevin. "But this is my life, you understand?"

The DON'T WALK changes to WALK, and Kevin and Lucy, well-trained New Yorkers, begin walking even though they are in the middle of a heated conversation. In New York you have to keep moving no matter what.

"You should be grateful to me," says Lucy as they continue up crowded and cold Second Avenue, "for helping you sever an unhealthy relationship."

"Grateful? My life is totally fucked, thanks to you."

"As I recall, your life has been totally fucked for as long as I've known you and the only reason I keep you for a friend is that you make my life look good by comparison."

"Thank you. That's very moving. Particularly coming from someone who has never sold a piece of art in her life, except to her own parents."

This genuinely hurts Lucy. For the most part, she can dish it out better than she can take it, especially when it comes to her art, and also she remembers how good their kiss was, and it feels like it happened a hundred years ago. She feels like she wants to cry, but she fights back her tears, and says, "Well, since I clearly don't measure up to your high standards, maybe I should just leave."

"Maybe you should!"

So Lucy turns around and heads back down Second, in the direction of Jack Dempsey's and Monica's party.

Kevin keeps walking also, but then he too remembers their kiss. "Where are you going?" he shouts after her.

"To find that bartender!" she screams over her shoulder.

This makes Kevin angry and jealous, so he shouts, "Well, give that ASSHOLE my regards!"

Lucy turns and screams, "Fuck you!" Then she spins around and walks as fast as she can.

Kevin, to show her that he's not following her, though she's not looking anyway, starts to walk backward and shouts, "Yeah? Fuck you too!"

But because he's stepping backward, he doesn't see where he's going and he knocks into a bucket filled with bouquets of roses that men in love are supposed to buy for their sweethearts on New Year's Eve. A large, homeless Vietnam vet has bought this bucket of roses and is trying to sell them at a profit. Kevin falls over the bucket, toppling it, and all the water spills out and Kevin lands on the roses, crushing most of them. He lies there on the sidewalk, in disbelief that he's fallen. He looks up at the sky in shock, but he also feels a certain calmness in just lying there, in just giving up on life. Then he feels something very cold—the icy water from the bucket is soaking his pants.

"Fuck!" he shouts. And then blocking his view of the black night sky is the unshaven and jaundiced face of a very unhappy Vietnam vet. But then the face smiles. A thought has come to it. The face says to Kevin, "You just bought six dozen roses, *asshole.*"

32

Bridget and Caitlyn are sitting at a table at the Big Island bar on Fourteenth Street. It is a Hawaiian-themed bar and is quite crowded. QB has gone to get them drinks. The girls don't speak. They just stare at each other.

Then QB arrives and the girls break out their best phony smiles. QB puts down three mai tais on the table. "So here we are," he says. And he takes the seat next to Bridget, which upsets Caitlyn, so she says nastily, "Don't you ever get tired of serving drinks?"

"Well . . . I got served at the bar . . . I only *carried* them here."

"I just love this place," says Bridget, wanting to score some points after Caitlyn's cutting remark. She feels she's way ahead, but why not put the game out of Caitlyn's reach?

"I work here on weekends," says QB.

"You're kidding," says Bridget, "I can't believe I haven't seen you here—"

"I'm here constantly," says Caitlyn, cutting Bridget off.

"I practically live here," says Bridget.

"So do I," says Caitlyn.

Bridget glares at Caitlyn, and pulls out a cigarette. Then she leans seductively into QB. "Do you have a light?" she asks. But before he can offer her one, Caitlyn quickly lights a match and puts it practically into Bridget's red hair, nearly lighting it on fire. Bridget pulls her head back and again dilates her nostrils at Caitlyn. Then she shoots her hand out and violently grabs Caitlyn's matches. She opens the matchbook to light her own cigarette and sees Caitlyn's name and number scrawled on the inside. She thinks this was intended for QB, not knowing it had originally been given to Eric. But she still thinks it's a bitchy maneuver. She coolly lights her cigarette and puts the matches in her purse.

QB, having witnessed this whole odd, hostile exchange between these two supposed friends, raises his glass, and says, hoping to smooth things over, "Well, here we are! Happy New Year."

"Cheers," says Caitlyn to QB, all sweet and syrupy.

"Yeah, right," says Bridget. And they all clink their glasses and drink.

QB, uncomfortable with the tension between these two, copes by starting to talk about himself. "I can tell you one thing. In a couple of years, I won't be serving mai tais anymore. There's a lot more I want to do with my life."

"Me too," says Bridget. "I'm an artist, but I spend most of

my time working as a receptionist for this stupid company."

"That's nothing," says Caitlyn. "I have to wait tables all week."

"So what would *you* rather be doing?" Bridget asks QB, pretending to play the attentive female.

"Law. Right now I'm in my second year of law school. Eighteen months to go and then no more bartending."

Both Bridget and Caitlyn are silenced by this. Then Caitlyn says, "Law school?"

"You're kidding, right?" says Bridget.

"No, I'm not. My dad's a lawyer and it seems to be something I have a feeling for. My plan is after a few years with a firm, maybe my dad's, I can go out on my own and devote myself full time to playing the market and buying and reselling converted co-op properties."

"You're not an actor?" asks Bridget.

QB laughs. "No, no way," he says.

Bridget and Caitlyn stare at one another. QB then begins to explain to them why real estate law is exciting, especially in New York City.

"Zoning laws, you know, building rights, are really fascinating. It can take years to get all the necessary permits . . . I spend hours poring over these books, it's really cool . . ."

33

Monica is lying on the floor of her apartment. It's a quarter to eleven and she still has only one guest—Eric. And he has convinced her to get down on her rug so that he can give her a soothing backrub, to take away all her troubles. He's hoping to demonstrate to her that he's a sensitive man, and he has the further hope that this massage session will lead to sex.

He straddles her back rather awkwardly and uses her ass as a seat. She grunts, but he doesn't take notice. He cracks his fingers like a concert pianist and then goes to work. He starts by massaging her shoulders, but does so in a brusque and unfeeling way. This is because he was not touched a great deal as a child. He was mostly raised by a cool nanny (his family was quite wealthy, thus his trust fund), and so he seems to be lacking any concept of tenderness or awareness of another person's body.

"How does this feel?" he asks. "Better, huh? See, it's all in the technique. Most people underestimate the importance of the downthrust." He tries to thrust down on Monica's shoulder blades; he vaguely remembers seeing a massage demonstration on *The Merv Griffin Show* when he was a young boy.

"Eric, you're hurting me," pleads Monica, trapped on her carpet by the downthrusting Eric.

"Oh, sorry," he says, and he tries another move. He lifts her by the face and digs his thumbs into her temples.

"Well, what about this?" he asks. "That feels good, right?"

"That's very painful!"

Eric, frustrated, drops her face, and her chin hits the rug and the hard floor beneath it. Eric destraddles her; he's impatient—he wants immediate positive feedback, and since he's not getting it he stands up, disgusted. He thinks she's a complainer and isn't trying to be receptive.

She sits up and rubs her face and chin and she feels kind of beat up, but the pain is good in that it momentarily distracts her from thinking about her failure of a New Year's Eve party.

"You know," says Eric, pacing back and forth, "I don't think I'm the one with the problem here. I think it's you. I think you're just blaming me for being bad in bed because you're not open to pleasure. A lot of women have trouble with orgasms."

She isn't sure where to begin to straighten this man out. "Listen, I don't have orgasm problems . . . And your problem . . . well, it's not anything you do really, it's . . . an *emotion.*"

"An emotion?"

"Yeah," she says, and she gets off her rug and sits down on one of her chairs. She's feeling very weary.

But Eric is still on fire, pacing. This word "emotion" is too vague for him. He needs answers *now!* "What the fuck is *emotion* supposed to mean?"

"I don't know—I can't describe it."

"Well, that's very helpful, thank you," he says, bitterly. "An *emotion!* You know, that's so typical of you women. It's all about *emotions,* it's all about *feelings* and *intimacy* and all that vague ambiguous bullshit. I mean, it's sex, okay? It's two people—in bed—getting off! Nothing more."

"You wanted to know why you were bad in bed, so I told you. You don't have to bite my head off just because you happen to be inadequate in this one particular area!"

"I'M NOT INADEQUATE!" Eric shouts, fighting for his life, and then, inspired, he begins to unbutton his shirt, and says to Monica, "Listen, you just get that goddamn dress off. I'll show you who's inadequate!"

Then Eric doesn't bother to get the rest of his buttons—he rips his shirt off and throws it to the floor.

"What are you doing?" Monica asks.

"What do you think I'm doing? I'm going to prove you wrong. That's right—I'm going to have you on your knees, sweetheart—begging for more."

He goes over to the food table and sweeps away bottles and dips and plates of crackers. The crab dip, miraculously, remains unharmed.

"Are you insane?" asks Monica, rushing over. "Stop it."

Eric responds to this question about his sanity by grabbing Monica's wrist. His bare chest is heaving. He's going to throw her on that table and have his way with her.

"Stop it, you asshole," she says. "What are you doing?" But before she can protest more, he kisses her full on the mouth, bending her at the waist and to his will. And it's the best kiss he has ever delivered in his life. It's full of passion and bravado and madness.

Monica finds herself giving in to it. Kisswise, he has hit a home run, and she hears the crowd cheering, she finds herself heating up, but then she pulls away.

"Eric—Jesus," she says, and she looks at the mess he's made on the floor.

"Get on the table," he says.

"Don't be ridiculous, help me clean up."

"Wasn't that a good kiss?"

"I don't care, you've wrecked my party."

"What party? I'm the party." Just then the doorbell rings.

"See! Oh, my God, a *guest* . . . Put your shirt on."

So Monica walks calmly to the door, restraining herself, wanting to have some dignity, and then she swings the door open, planning on greeting her guest with a big smile, but it's . . . Hillary, who looks past Monica and says, "Jesus. Nobody's here yet?"

"Eric's here," says Monica, trying to save some face.

"Eric, right!" says Hillary. This is the guy she's been promised. She walks past Monica, dumping her coat in Monica's arms, and approaches Eric, who has finished putting on his ripped shirt.

"Hi, I'm Hillary. I saw your flower paintings. I just loved them. You're really talented." Hillary decides to use the direct super-flattery approach to seduction, which usually works quite well with men. Compliment them enough and they're yours. They all want a woman's (i.e., Mommy's) approval.

"My flower paintings?"

Hillary puts her arm through Eric's and leads him to sit down on the couch so that she can have him all to herself. She calls out to Monica, "How about some music?"

Monica takes Hillary's coat and walks across her loft and throws it onto the floor of her bedroom and then gives the coat a kick for good measure. Then she goes to the stereo and puts the Bing Crosby record back on. Just for Eric. For good measure.

34

QB excuses himself to go to the bathroom, and Bridget and Caitlyn, without saying a word, but in perfect sync, put on their coats and steal out of the bar. They quickly head up Fourteenth Street. Bridget is aggravated. "Well, that was a total waste of time," she says.

"Really—law school. I'm sorry, but that is so unbelievably dull," says Caitlyn.

The girls are no longer enemies. Their friendship has been reestablished by the presence of a common enemy—the Boring Male.

"And do you believe him going on about real estate?" says Bridget.

"What is it with guys that they think we give a shit about their stuff?" And just as she says this, Caitlyn has a preternatural sense of something dangerous behind her: She glances over her shoulder to see QB emerging from the bar.

"There he is!" whispers Caitlyn, and she grabs Bridget and they duck into the doorway of a Mexican restaurant. QB doesn't see them. His downfield vision is poor from too much law study. The two friends press themselves tightly against the door of the darkened restaurant.

"You think this is too mean ditching him this way?" whispers Bridget.

"Please. What does he think, we'll just be waiting for him to get back from the bathroom so he can keep going on about the economy?"

"And I can't believe he was going to take us to the same party that Eric was going to. The whole world must be going there." QB had told them the address of the party at the Big Island and the girls were shocked by the coincidence.

QB continues to scan the street. He is angry and confused. *I can't believe they snuck out on me. I thought we were going to have a threesome or something.* He goes back into the bar. *When I have my degree shit like this won't happen.*

Caitlyn pokes her head out of the doorway—the coast is clear. She and Bridget begin walking west on Fourteenth. Bridget removes the matchbook from her purse and hands it to Caitlyn, and says, "By the way, next time you might want to try a new approach. This thing with the matchbook is so predictable."

"What do you expect? I'm under a deadline here."

"What time is it, anyway?"

Caitlyn looks at her watch. "Oh, my God!"

"What?"

"We've got one hour."

Bridget is horrified. "One hour . . . are you serious? We're going to be jinxed the whole year!!!"

Caitlyn grabs Bridget by the arm. "Let's get a cab!" But there are no cabs available. They start to run. They reach First Avenue, but it goes uptown and they want to go downtown. "Let's get a taxi at Second Avenue and get to that party," Caitlyn cries. "It's our only hope!"

"I can't believe that boring lawyer dragged us all the way to Fourteenth Street," says Bridget. "I hate Fourteenth Street and that bar sucked!"

They run, but it's a long run. They keep looking for taxis along Fourteenth but there are no free ones, and the crosstown block between First and Second Avenues is endless. They feel like they are running forever, and the clock is ticking on these two young ladies. A yearlong jinx hangs over their heads like a guillotine, and Caitlyn's diaphragm in her purse is as heavy as a Manhattan phone book, one without a single number of a man she can sleep with.

35

Jack and Cindy emerge out of the alleyway and onto Sixth Street. They are holding hands. Jack directs them back toward Second Avenue and the party. Everything feels all right; what else could go wrong? And then the what else goes wrong. Coming out of Gandhi II and headed right for Jack and Cindy is Cheryl with a backup squad of five single women.

But they don't spot their prey, and Jack alertly yanks Cindy into the doorway of another Indian restaurant, the Rose of India.

"Hey, what are you doing?" asks Cindy.

"Nothing," he says, and then thinking fast and executing the best way to shut her up, leans in and gives her a good long kiss. When they part, she is smiling dreamily.

"Jack, that was nice," she says, and just then the angry Cheryl-led lynch mob passes the Rose of India, and Jack grabs Cindy again in a kiss, keeping her between him and his pursuers. Cindy's eyes are closed in bliss, but Jack's eyes are open, watching the mob continue down the street. Then they abruptly turn around, sensing that they have gone in the wrong direction, and so they head back toward Second. Jack keeps the kiss going. Cindy is in heaven. The posse goes right past Jack for the second time.

Jack counts to twenty in his mind, and then, thinking it's safe, he breaks the kiss, and peers up Sixth. The posse is at Second, looking up and down the avenue. Jack turns to Cindy, who is just standing there, eyes still closed, hoping for another smooch.

"Are you okay?" Jack asks.

"Wow, that was delicious," she says.

"Good, good. I liked it, too . . . Let's walk some more." He takes her by the hand and leads her to First Avenue, away from his angry pursuers. It's been a night of close escapes.

"I guess I was wrong about tonight turning out to be so terrible," Cindy says.

"Yeah, it's been great," says Jack, just glad he avoided a crazy confrontation with Cheryl. "Now we'll go to the party and bring in the New Year."

Cindy is still all flushed from their kissing in the doorway of the Rose of India, and she likes holding Jack's hand, and she feels overwhelmed with emotion. "Jack," she says, "I know it's sudden but I . . . I think I'm falling in love with you."

Jack is horrified. *I can't believe she said "love." This is ridiculous.* He gives her hand a little squeeze to acknowledge what she has said, but he's really hoping that she'll just drop the whole thing.

They reach First Avenue and take a right, heading south. Jack gives a quick look back down Sixth Street, but they seem to have completely lost his pursuers.

He and Cindy walk to Fifth Street without talking, but Cindy, who's been waiting for a response to her proclamation—something more than a hand squeeze—can't take Jack's silence, so she stops them on the sidewalk.

"Did you hear what I said?" she asks sweetly, smiling at him. "I think I love you."

"Not again," Jack mutters.

"Not again? What do you mean?"

"Nothing . . . you just . . . don't do this, okay? You don't even know me!"

"But I like you and I thought that you . . . I thought that you liked me, too."

"Well, I . . . I like you a lot. But I like lots of people . . ."

Jack and Cindy are already, on their first official date, in that strange and mystifying place—The Relationship Zone. They hardly know one another but they are behaving like classic examples of their respective sexes. Cindy loves Jack for three reasons: (1) he does have a sweet nature—there's an endearing quality to his eyes, a gentleness; (2) he's good-looking, sturdy, and strong, and he possesses a certain animal magnetism—women like the way he smells; and (3) Jack is entirely remote, unattainable, unreachable, and unavailable. He is simply Un.

So number two, the smell factor, and number three are the most important, especially number three. Jack reminds women of their fathers. They can't get his love. He's distracted. This drives them wild. They want to get his love. He is like a math problem that remains unsolved for centuries; and mathematicians will spend their whole lives trying to undo such a riddle. Usually failing. So it is with women. They will spend their whole lives trying to undo the mystery of a man like Jack. It is a love of riddles that began with their first riddle, their first unavailable man—Daddy.

Jack, as a classic male in The Relationship Zone, hates the word "love." Women use it so easily. They try to pin him down with it. He has no idea what they are talking about. He does *like* them. Feels, at times, comforted by them. Enjoys very much being flattered by them and sleeping with them. But he doesn't feel love.

He's never really felt love, except when he was very little and first starting school and his mother took him to kindergarten every morning those first few weeks, but he couldn't stop crying. So then he experienced love, but he experienced it as pain. The pain of Mommy's withdrawal. But eventually, he learned to cope. He learned that he didn't need Mommy. And he didn't cry anymore when she left him at school.

And now, at the age of twenty-seven, Jack doesn't really need anyone. He just needs himself. And he may not fall in love, until he finds a woman who for some reason he *needs;* the way he once needed, deep in his soul, his mother. But right now he's very much a young male, a lone wolf, really. He just wants to feel free. Free to do what he wants. And so what he doesn't want is to be pinned down. He doesn't want to take care of these girls who tell him they love him. He doesn't like hurting them, but it happens over and over again, and he always thinks he'll stay away from women, but he can't . . .

So there we have it: The Relationship Zone. Confusing. Baffling. The stuff of poetry, songs, and self-help best-sellers.

Cindy looks like she's on the verge of tears. Jack expects this and yet dreads it. He hates it when they cry. It breaks his heart. Makes him hate himself.

"Come on, don't cry," he says. And then he commits a terrible, terrible faux pas—but it has been a stressful night. He says, "Don't cry, Cheryl." The name that had earlier escaped him during his fit of Name Lock now comes out. It's the dreaded Current Lover/Ex-Lover Mistaken Name Switch—or its other, more simple name: Death Wish.

"Cheryl!" says Cindy, and out come the tears. "I'm Cindy." She has given Jack her virginity and a proclamation of love from her heart and he doesn't know her name. The tears really flow now.

"I'm sorry," Jack pleads.

"Who's Cheryl?" Cindy asks through her tears.

A girl who wants to have me killed. "Nobody," he says.

"You're in love with this Cheryl person, aren't you?"

"God, no! . . . I'm not in love with anybody. To be perfectly honest, the whole topic makes me uncomfortable . . . Why can't we just go slow? A person shouldn't say the word 'love' for at least a year. So can't we just slow down? Get back to being on a date and go to this party?"

"I wouldn't go to that party with you if you were the last man on earth!" Cindy is still outraged that this idiot called her Cheryl, and that he's completely unromantic. Waiting one year to say "love"! The heart knows no timetable!

So she begins to walk away from Jack, but her equilibrium

and coordination, still thrown off by her loss of hymen the night before, causes her to step on some ice near the curb and she then slips and falls on her ass right next to a parking meter.

Jack runs to her. "Are you okay?"

"Oh, God . . . Oh, God," Cindy moans. A few people gather around the fallen person. It is human nature to form a crowd and gawk when a fellow human injures themself.

"Have you broken something?" Jack asks.

"Only the heel of my shoe," she says. "But I think I fell right in some dog shit." Some dog had not only decided to pee on a parking meter, but to take a dump there as well, and not too long ago, because the shit, unfortunately for Cindy, had not yet frozen.

Jack helps Cindy up, and, sure enough, the back of her coat, right in her own buttocks area, is smeared with dog crap. Several of the concerned, voyeuristic bystanders giggle and move on.

"This is so embarrassing!" Cindy yells, while swiveling her neck around so that she can see the dog shit. "I hate my life!"

"It's okay," says Jack. "It's not so bad." He tries to touch her shoulder, to comfort her, but she recoils from him.

"Leave me alone. I hate you. You're a big phony. You're not nice at all."

"I never said I was nice. You're the one who kept going on about how nice I am."

"You're so conceited!" Passersby, smelling a fight, rubberneck, slowing down the foot traffic on the sidewalk. For an injury, they stop completely, but for a fight they merely slow down, not wanting to get caught in any cross fire.

"What are you talking about?" asks Jack. He hates being

called conceited. Whenever girls turn on him they say two things: "You don't listen" and "You're conceited."

"You think I haven't noticed?" Cindy says. "All night you've been hounding me for a reason—why did I choose you? What was it exactly about you? You, you, you! That's all you care about!"

"I was curious!" Jack says.

"You think there's something special about you? Well, guess what—it could've been anybody!" Cindy sees that this hurts Jack, it registers on his face like a slap. She continues, she's got the momentum now, even if her heel is broken and her coat is covered in dog shit. "That's right! You were there, that's all. I just wanted to get it over with! I would've gone home with anybody last night . . . it could've been anybody!"

Now, this is meant to be a slam at Jack, and it is, but it's not something Cindy really should be boasting about. Would she really have gone home with anybody? No. Jack had those aforementioned fatherlike qualities—unattainable, unreachable, and unavailable. The truth is, many men have those qualities, but not all men. So it couldn't have been anybody, and Cindy knows this, but she wants to hurt Jack and she's managed to do so.

Jack hangs his head. He always wishes that he could end things with girls and that their memory of him would be a good one, but most times it's like this. For it to end, their love has to turn to hate.

He takes a breath and looks at her. He's going to cut his losses and bring this thing to a close.

"Well, I guess it's all come out now," he says, calmly. "So why don't we just end this date, right here, right now?"

"That's fine with me," says Cindy.

"We'll just each go home and hopefully we'll never see each other again."

"That sounds perfect."

"But just to be nice, even though I'm not nice, I will be a gentleman and hail you a cab so that you get home safely. Is that all right?"

"Yes," she says.

Jack steps onto First Avenue and puts out his hand. There's plenty of traffic, but no available cabs.

"I bet that Cheryl hates you, too," says Cindy.

Jack keeps holding out his hand for a taxi. A stoic male. "Yeah, she hates me," he says. "Cheryl and every other girl in New York City."

36

Stephie is standing all by herself at the party on Avenue D. They eventually left the Ugly Dog and came here to find Tony and deliver the package. The party is in a windowless basement apartment. About one hundred people are crammed into a room about the size of half a basketball court. The smoke is so thick and the music so loud that it's like standing behind the exhaust pipe of a jet plane about to take off. The crowd is a scary mix—for Stephie—of bikers, punks, and drug-addict types (to Stephie's eyes).

So she leans against a wall, wondering when this night will come to an end. Tom, meanwhile, has gone off to find Tony, and Val and Dave are in the middle of the room dancing. Val has now seemingly switched her affections toward the large, man-of-few-words Dave. Stephie watches Dave offer Val a little pill. To

Stephie's horror, Val takes it and then Dave takes one. Stephie is further horrified when she watches Dave and Val begin to make out. Stephie knew Val was wild, that she went further than anybody else with guys back in Ronkonkoma, but tonight is unprecedented—making out with *two* guys, two roadies for Roadkill. And Dave is *gross*.

Stephie, scared, yet bored, looks down at her boots, and is happy to see that the wet one has dried and there doesn't appear to be any stain. *Thank God for small gifts.* So, feeling a little better, she looks up, and two biker guys from across the room hold up—for her to see—a bottle of Jack Daniel's. They are in Hell's Angels jackets and they have beards, and they pantomime that she should share the bottle with them. And then they begin to struggle through the crowd to get to her. But she didn't nod yes or no, she was too petrified. As they get nearer, she thinks she hears one of them say, "Young blood."

With that she bolts for the door, gets out into the basement hallway, and hides under the staircase. The two bikers emerge from the party, don't see her, figure she's left altogether, and so they go back into the party looking for somebody else to share their bottle.

It's dank and creepy under the staircase, so Stephie comes out and sits on the cold concrete stairs. She wraps her arms around her knees and bows her head down. She feels like her old heroine Dorothy. *I just want to go home. I just want to go home. I just want to go home.* And then, like Dorothy, she closes her eyes and clicks the heels of her boots together, wishing crazily for a miracle.

When she opens her eyes, hoping to see her living room in Ronkonkoma, she instead sees Tom and she's startled, so she lets out a yelp.

"What's the matter?" asks Tom. He has two beers and the package.

"Nothing," says Stephie. "You just scared me to death, that's all."

"You want a beer?" asks Tom.

"Okay," says Stephie.

"Can I sit next to you?"

"All right," she says, grudgingly, and she scoots over so that Tom can join her on the stair. He opens up a beer and hands it to her. She takes a sip and says, "How come you still got that package? I thought we were getting out of here already."

"Tony isn't here yet. We have to wait and see if he shows up."

"Great."

They sit in silence, sipping their beers. Tom makes an attempt at conversation. He's a big guy, a little rough around the edges, but he has a sweet side.

So he says to Stephie, "Cool party, right?"

"It sucks. I want to leave."

The conversation dies out quick. Tom attempts a little jump start. "So where would you like to go?"

"Ronkonkoma."

"Where's that? Japan?"

"No. God. Long Island. Where me and Val are from."

"Long Island. I hear it's nice out there. I'm from Jersey."

This perks Stephie up a little. "I'm a big fan of the Boss," she says.

"Yeah, he's all right. But when you're from Jersey he kind of gets shoved down your throat."

Stephie looks at him coolly. The conversation dies out

again. They sip their beers. Then Tom screws up the courage and says, "So, can I ask you something?"

"It's a free country."

"Did Val say anything to you about me? Because, you know, I thought we were really hitting it off there for a while." Stephie looks at Tom, she really doesn't want to hear this. But he's just staring at his beer, peeling off the label, and he says, continuing, "I mean, I thought she really liked me . . . But now she's in there making out with Dave, and I'm just wondering if maybe I did something to offend her."

Stephie has no idea what's going through Val's mind. "I don't know if you offended her," she says. "Probably not, she's just partying."

"It's like, when I first met her, I thought, whoa, this is it . . . You know what I mean? This is the one. Because the thing about Val, she's different. She's got all this energy, like a little girl or something. Like you want to take care of her in a way. Look out for her, you know what I mean?"

Stephie looks at Tom. *Is this guy for real? He's a roadie for Roadkill, but he's all gushy when it comes to Val.*

Tom looks away from Stephie; he feels self-conscious. "I guess," he says, "you think I'm crazy talking like that about a girl I just met."

Then he looks back at Stephie. His brow is furrowed and his large brown eyes have a vulnerable cast to them. Stephie feels bad for him. She even wonders if *she* should kiss him. But then all *her* troubles and horrors and fears take precedence in her mind, and she says, "Can I tell *you* something?" Tom nods his head. "This is the worst night of my life. The worst. I'm in a basement on fucking Avenue D. All night long weird shit has been happening. I never should have come in to the city. I'd like to never come here again . . . So I'm sorry if Val hurt your feelings. I'm sorry you're having trouble finding the right girl. But I'm just trying to get home before somebody kills me, okay? I think that's a lot worse than being wrong about Val."

Stephie's speech kills their conversation for good. Tom says, "I hear what you're saying," and then they just sit there in silence drinking their beers. They've taken their problems back into themselves. Tom's got heartbreak and Stephie's got homesickness.

37

Kevin, luckily, has just enough money to buy all the roses from the Vietnam vet. He then goes down Second Avenue looking for Lucy. He finds her in Jack Dempsey's. She went back there hoping to find the bartender, even though it's after eleven, well past the end of his shift.

She's at the bar as Kevin approaches. Her back is to him, and he feels a wave of tenderness seeing her there alone, smoking a cigarette. Her shoulders look thin and vulnerable. He'd like to put his arms around her, have her bury her sweet face in his chest.

To be romantic and playful, he waves the flowers in front of her. She turns and sees that Kevin is the man offering the roses, and so she looks away, uninterested and disgusted. She sips her drink. She takes a drag of her cigarette. Kevin withdraws the flowers, holds them to his chest.

"I brought you these roses," he says.

Lucy nods, unimpressed. She is more interested in her cigarette. Kevin looks at the open stool next to her. "Mind if I sit down?" he asks.

"I'm with someone," she says, coolly. "You understand?"

"You're with someone?"

"That's right."

"Not that bartender, I hope?"

"He's on the phone, calling his parents to wish them Happy New Year. He's a good guy. He'll be right back."

QB, after getting blown off by Bridget and Caitlyn, felt too embarrassed to stay at the Big Island bar and so he decided to come back to Jack Dempsey's to ring in the New Year, where he's been happily reunited with Lucy.

And so Kevin just stands at the bar, feeling foolish with his armful of roses.

"You can just go home now like you wanted to," says Lucy. "You don't have to worry about me at all. My New Year's is set."

Kevin looks to see if the bartender is headed their way. He doesn't see the guy. "You don't even know this bartender," says Kevin.

"So?"

"So it just seems a little . . . I don't know . . . sudden or something, to just be going off with him."

"You know, you're much more judgmental between girlfriends. Have you ever noticed that? Since when do you care how quickly I pick somebody up?"

Once again, for the umpteenth time this evening, Kevin and Lucy are pissing each other off. "Fine," says Kevin, "throw yourself at some stranger just because he's good-looking. That's your business. I'm going home, where I should have been all along."

So Kevin heads for the door, angry. Then he remembers the roses. He returns to Lucy and puts them down hard on the bar in front of her. It's quite a lot of roses. "Here, enjoy," says Kevin.

"Thank you, lover boy," says Lucy, and she puts her lips together as if she was Marilyn Monroe and she makes a big, wet, sarcastic kissing sound.

Kevin walks off again, furious, gets outside and takes a few steps and then stops. He doesn't really want to go home, and he looks at all the windows of the apartment buildings, and he thinks how behind every window there is a stranger. And he wonders how many of these strangers are having sex. It's a whole city of strangers and then two things become clear to him: He doesn't want to be alone, and, more than that, he wants to be with Lucy.

He goes back into the bar. Lucy's smoking another cigarette, the stool next to her remains empty. Turns out QB is something of a mama's boy; he's still on the phone with her.

Kevin sits on the stool and Lucy turns, expecting the bartender.

"Jesus," she says. "This is like déjà vu."

"Lucy, listen to me . . . there's something I want to say . . ." He hesitates.

"What, already?"

"Well . . ."

"Come on, just spit it out."

"Let's do it."

"What?"

"I think we should go back to the Kiev and do it in the bathroom. We'll just go back in time, start over."

"You've got to be kidding."

"I'm not. Let's go back there right now. We started something good in there." Kevin looks at Lucy; he's alluding to their kiss. He knows that *she* felt something. She knows that *he* felt something.

"Kevin, this is too weird," she says. "We're driving each other crazy tonight. Let's just stop, all right? And I can't just ditch this bartender."

"It's my birthday, remember? We're obligated to do it. You said so yourself." Kevin holds out his hand. Lucy looks at it. She feels a tumble in her stomach. A tumble of nerves, of happiness. "Come on, I dare you," says Kevin.

She puts her hand in his and smiles. Then she gets her coat on and they leave.

QB hangs up the phone, which is at the end of the bar next to the bathrooms, and he walks back over to where he was sitting with Lucy. She's gone and her coat is gone. If she had gone to the ladies' room he would have seen her. He stares at the roses, which have been left behind. Are they some kind of thanks-but-no-thanks gesture? He can't figure out what's happening. He's been dumped twice in one night. Nothing like this has ever occurred before. He doesn't understand it. He cups his hand in front of his mouth and checks his breath. *It doesn't seem bad.* He goes to the bathroom to see if there are any snots hanging out of his nose. He looks in the mirror and gives his nostrils a thorough inspection. *All clear . . . this is a fucked-up night.*

38

It's 11:25 and Monica still has only two guests: her ex-boyfriend Eric and her so-called friend Hillary.

Hillary and Eric are sitting on the couch engrossed in conversation about the artist Steinmetz. Monica is on the other side of the room staring at the buffet table, which she has reassembled, as best she can, after Eric cleared it off. She thinks how he wanted to take her, right on the table. It now sort of thrills her, and that kiss he gave her was pretty good. But there's nothing she can do about it. Hillary is fully exercising her part of the deal—she came back, thus she gets Eric.

So now Monica is just staring at her table of food, drinking far too much wine, and listening to every word of Hillary and Eric's conversation. She mouths Hillary's overly solicitous, flirtatious responses. Women hate to observe other women's techniques of seduction. It's a reflection of themselves that's too glaring. And why don't the men ever see what's happening? It's beyond obvious. So it's killing Monica to listen to Hillary pander to Eric, and she guzzles more wine to deal with it. *Listen to that bullshit. She's throwing herself at him, what a slut, and he thinks they're talking about art.*

"I'm really impressed that you know Steinmetz's work," says Eric to Hillary. "Not too many people know him, and even fewer like him. I'm a huge fan."

"Oh, I love his work. I adore it."

"You know, I believe he's influenced me more than any other artist."

"Well, I think he's a genius," says Hillary.

Monica finishes her glass, and then refills it. This discussion of Steinmetz goes on for another ten minutes. No new guests have arrived. Monica has polished off a bottle in the last half hour alone, and before that she had drunk a bottle's worth. She is now at the very beginning of bottle three, and is thoroughly inebriated, almost to the point of blacking out. She's so drunk that she's only vaguely aware that she's in tremendous pain over two things: (1) her profound lack of popularity—no one has come to her New Year's Eve party, and she must have invited two hundred people; and (2) the torture of having to listen to Hillary try to get into Eric's pants.

She grips the buffet table to steady herself.

"I also like his photographic work," says Eric. "What's so interesting is the way the model is used. She's as much accomplice as subject."

"That's very perceptive of you," says Hillary, smiling at Eric, touching his knee. "I never thought of it that way."

Eric is flattered. He continues his critique: "It's this confusion of whether the woman is accomplice or subject that draws the viewer in. Are we voyeurs or are we being looked at?"

"Like the *Mona Lisa* looks at us, right?"

"Yeah, that's interesting."

Monica takes a carrot stick and writes a message in the crab dip: "Help Me." But her writing is shaky, because of her drunkenness, and crab dip doesn't make the best writing tablet.

"So you've seen his new show, right?" asks Hillary.

"Actually, I haven't yet. I feel embarrassed."

"I saw it, it's amazing. It affected my dreams."

"Maybe I'll see it on Saturday," says Eric.

"I'd even go see it again. Steinmetz is so inspiring."

Monica crosses out "Help Me" and begins to write in the crab dip, "I want to die."

"You'd see it again?" asks Eric.

"Of course."

"Would you like to go see it with me?" Eric asks shyly, bashfully.

"Really? Okay. I'd love to . . . Wow . . . that would be great." Hillary gives Eric her most beguiling and becoming smile. Monica finishes her sentence in the crab dip and catches the look on Hillary's face. The hook has been set in Eric's mouth. He's all hers. Monica is revolted. Then she stares at her pathetic, empty loft. The room begins to spin. In the middle of the cyclone, she sees Eric lean forward and kiss Hillary. Monica puts the carrot stick in her mouth, pretends it's a gun and says, "Bang." And whether it's the booze or a self-induced faint, it doesn't matter, because Monica can't take any more of this night and she crumples to the ground, passed out. Her crab-covered carrot stick, like a suicide revolver, falls out of her hand. Hillary and Eric rush to her. She's okay, but they can't wake her up. It's 11:43 P.M., seventeen minutes to New Year's.

Monica's doorbell begins to ring.

39

Jack is still trying to hail a cab for Cindy, who stands on First Avenue, trying to maintain her dignity with dog shit on the back of her coat.

Jack finally spots an empty cab, which has smoke and disco music pouring out of the crack in the driver's-side window. It's the dreadlocked driver who earlier in the night had chauffeured Kevin and Lucy. But he's rather stoned and lost in his music, and he doesn't hear Jack's cry of "Taxi!" And so he continues barreling up First Avenue.

"Just drive on by like I'm nothing," shouts Jack, and he feels like giving up. He looks at Cindy, who is purposely not looking at him. "Can I try to explain something?" asks Jack.

"I'm not speaking to you," says Cindy. "Remember—this date is over."

"Well, what was that?" asks Jack. "You spoke to me to tell me you're not speaking to me . . . I think if you hear me out, you might feel better."

Cindy looks at him and barely nods her head, giving him the okay. Jack comes off the street and onto the sidewalk, stands next to Cindy.

"See, what happened between us," Jack begins, "is like this continuing problem with me. It happens all the time. I meet a woman, we go home together, everything seems fine, but then, the next day . . ."

"The next day what?" Cindy asks.

"Suddenly they tell me they've developed these . . . *feelings* for me."

"So what are you saying? Every woman you go to bed with falls in love with you or something?"

"It's like this curse. It never ends."

"Women fall in love with you, and you think that's a curse?"

"You have no idea."

"No, I don't. Because I think you're lucky. There are some people who wait their whole lives for someone to say they feel that way about them—and you just throw it away like it's nothing, like it's just this minor inconvenience! Well, you know something? You are cursed, Jack—but not the way you think!"

Jack stares at Cindy. Her hair, which she had tried to pile up at the start of the evening, is now completely down, but quite beautiful—it flows around her shoulders. She looks strong, clearheaded. She's becoming a woman.

"Good-bye, Jack," she says, and she crosses Sixth Street,

with all its Indian restaurants, and she hobbles proudly on her one good heel. Then she stops, takes her good shoe and snaps the heel off, and slam-dunks it into a garbage can. Walking evenly now, she steps out into First Avenue, raises her hand, and to Jack's great surprise, immediately hails a cab.

She gets in and—without knowing it—slams the door on part of her white cocktail dress (her loss-of-virginity-induced clumsiness is still a little in play). Jack watches the cab take off, the tail of the dress waving good-bye to him like a flag. He wonders what he has lost. He's left alone on the cold street.

40

Bridget and Caitlyn are huffing their way up Fourteenth Street. They're almost to Second Avenue. Bridget is in the lead, and looks over her shoulder and shouts at Caitlyn, "Will you hurry up? There's got to be a cab somewhere."

Caitlyn stops, bends over, and puts her hands on her knees. "I can't, I can't go on!"

Bridget doubles back and grabs Caitlyn's arm. "You listen to me! I am getting to that party, you understand? It's my only hope because of you!"

"Let's just give up. That party won't be any good."

"Who knows? But at least Eric will probably be there." Bridget starts running again.

"Eric?" shouts Caitlyn, and she too begins to run.

Bridget looks over her shoulder. She knows what's motivating Caitlyn. "Fine," she says. "You want Eric? I'll take the lawyer. I bet he shows up."

They get to Second Avenue, and suddenly there appears a cab. It's the dreadlocked driver. He missed Jack on First Avenue, made it all the way up to Fourteenth Street without a fare, and now is coming back down Second Avenue. He spots a gray-haired older woman hailing him and he pulls over. The woman is carrying a cat in a cat-case. Bridget sees this and dashes in front of the woman.

"I need this taxi," says Bridget. "If you try to get in I'll kill you."

"I'll call the police," says the woman. "I need to get home. My pussy is freezing."

Caitlyn arrives and says, "To hell with your cat. We have an emergency."

And the two girls bully the woman, intimidate her, and she steps back onto the avenue, frightened. Her cat peers out at the two desperate girls and meows and them vomits up a fur ball, because it's cold and nervous. Bridget opens the taxi door and slides in; Caitlyn follows. The driver, because of his loud disco music, hasn't heard a word of the exchange between the girls and the woman. He wonders for a moment about the old lady, but he doesn't really care. Also, he'd rather have these two fine-looking women in his cab.

"Twenty-one Great Jones Street," shouts Bridget over the music, "and please hurry."

The cab pulls out and gets to Thirteenth Street, but there traffic slows to a real New Year's Eve bumper-to-bumper snarl. The midnight hour is approaching.

Caitlyn glances out the back window to the old woman and

her cat-case. The old lady flashes her the finger. Caitlyn flips her back, then says to Bridget, "I can't believe you're so desperate that you'd go after that lawyer."

"Oh, I suppose now you want him for yourself?"

"You are so paranoid!" says Caitlyn.

"Or maybe you'd like Eric *and* the lawyer. Is that it?"

The cab crawls to Twelfth Street and comes to a complete halt. "Hey," Caitlyn says to the driver, "do you think you could move a little faster?"

"Sometimes you have to stay where you are to move forward," says the cabbie, feeling philosophical because of all the joints he's smoked.

"What did he say?" asks Bridget.

The cabbie lowers the music. He turns to the girls and offers each of them a handful of cigarettes.

"You two smoke?"

"Yeah," says Bridget.

"Here, have these cigarettes," says the cabbie. "They're Marlboro. I don't smoke cigarettes. But this guy left a whole carton in here. It was his birthday present. I'm trying to give away the whole thing—two hundred cigarettes—but to lots of people. You know, spread the wealth. A special New Year's Eve treat for being in my cab. You can even smoke *in the cab.* Tonight, I'm breaking my own rules."

"Thanks," says Bridget.

"Yeah, thank you," says Caitlyn, and she takes out her special matchbook that Bridget gave back to her, and she lights two cigarettes, one for herself and one for Bridget.

They make it to Eleventh Street and a disco song about a love triangle comes to an end, and the cabbie says, "You know, this song reminds me of an experience I had with a friend of mine. We were both in love with the same girl but he's the one who got her. Then one night, while he was sitting in a restaurant with the girl of my dreams, my friend choked to death on a string bean. I say to myself, 'Could it have been me choking on that string bean?' That's what I think of when I hear this song."

"So he's saying love kills?" asks Bridget, not addressing the driver, which often happens to cabbies.

"No, he's saying we shouldn't fight over these guys—and, personally, I think he's right."

The cabbie, who had heard their argument when they first got in the cab, had used the song as a way to lecture these girls. His mission this New Year's Eve, he feels, is to help people, show them how to be happy, *and* to give them cigarettes.

"Of course I'm right," he says. "Good friends have to stick together. They can't be divided by going after the same people of the opposite sex." He smiles at the girls in his rearview mirror.

"He's right," says Caitlyn, "we're best friends. We shouldn't keep letting these guys come between us."

"Yeah, but how can we stop?" asks Bridget.

"What if, for the sake of our friendship, we each agree to leave the party tonight alone?"

"So we don't get guys and just go home alone, even if it means we're jinxed for the whole year?"

"Right," says Caitlyn, "because tonight we learn not to compete with each other. It's like the start of a resolution. Like quitting smoking. And tonight is our first test of no more competing. I think it's a sacrifice we have to make for the sake of our friendship."

Bridget feels that Caitlyn, for once, is being sincere. Also, if they don't make this deal and Caitlyn gets lucky and Bridget doesn't, it would be a double jinx for the year. *This way Caitlyn doesn't get a guy, and I don't get one either, but at least there's no threat of the double jinx.*

"All right, for our friendship, I'll do it," says Bridget. "But you have to swear you'll do it."

"I swear," says Caitlyn. Then the two girls shake on it and give each other air kisses next to their cheeks. Then they lapse into silence and smoke their cigarettes.

"What you two are doing is beautiful," says the cabbie, taking a hit off his joint. Then he exhales the smoke and looks in the rearview mirror. Bridget happens to be glancing out the window; she's a little nervous about this deal. But Caitlyn meets the cabbie's eye in the mirror and unseen by Bridget gives him a loaded-with-innuendo smile. The cabbie is surprised, but he is also intrigued, and Caitlyn fingers her matchbook with her number inside.

41

Val and Stephie and Tom are dragging Dave up Third Street. Dave passed out at the party. The pill he took, intended to speed him up, actually slowed him down and he collapsed on the dance floor. Val, having a more rugged constitution, has hardly been affected by the pill. She and Stephie have one of Dave's arms and Tom has the other, and he also has the package for Tony, who never showed up.

The three of them are hoping to find a cab to get Dave back to his squatter's apartment, but there aren't many cabs in Alphabet City. As they drag Dave, a series of gunshots are heard nearby. Stephie's eyes widen. She wants to abandon Dave and just run.

"This guy weighs a ton," she says. "Let's just leave him and get the hell out of here."

"I'm not doing that to my friend," says Tom.

"We're never gonna make it out of here alive. Do you hear those gunshots?"

"They sound far away," says Val. "At least a block."

"Oh, that's real far, Val," says Stephie.

They drag Dave another few feet, and Stephie looks up and sees a street sign. "Oh, my God," she says gleefully, "it's B!" For Stephie, B is now so much better than D (death) and C (crazed killers).

She lets go of Dave and runs to the street sign and hugs it. "I never thought I'd be so glad to reach B."

Tom and Val drag Dave past Stephie and her new love, the street sign, and they get him onto a bench in front of a laundromat.

"Let's just put him in a cab," says Tom.

"We can't just put him in a cab. We have to wait till he's conscious," says Val, as Stephie approaches.

"That's very caring of you," says Tom, in a rare sarcastic moment—he's still hurt that Val was making out with Dave at the Avenue D party.

"Look, he'll be okay," says Stephie. "We'll just pay the driver and give him the address. Dave will wake up once he's in a car. Does he have any money?"

"Yeah, in his wallet," says Tom.

Stephie and Val begin to search around in Dave's pockets. Stephie finds several hot-dog and candy-bar wrappers and the peeled-off labels of beers, but no wallet.

"I'm not finding a wallet here," says Stephie. She feels inside his jacket. Dave is all hot and fat. "This guy's a whale," she says.

"Wait a minute," says Val. "I found it!" She pulls out a grungy blue Velcro-strapped surfer wallet and goes through it. "Hey, there's no money in here!"

"That's great," says Stephie. "Didn't I tell you we should have just left him behind?"

This pisses Tom off. This girl has been nothing but a whiny brat all night. "You know, Stephie," he says, "all you've been doing is complaining how horrible everything is, and I'm getting pretty sick of hearing it, you know."

Stephie looks at him, surprised, it's like cold water thrown in her face, and Val is just glad that somebody else is giving Stephie a piece of their mind.

"I mean," says Tom, "did you ever think to look on the bright side of things? Did you ever think, 'Hey, maybe I could have a good time if I shut my mouth for five seconds'? Jeez, nothing's ever good enough for you. Do you realize what a pain in the ass you are? . . . What's your problem, anyway?"

Stephie doesn't know what to say. It dawns on her that she hasn't been raped and that nothing bad has actually happened to her—except putting her foot in the toilet—and yet she's been acting like she's been in Vietnam.

"Sorry," she mumbles.

Val, meanwhile, has continued to look through Dave's wallet, just being snoopy, and she suddenly exclaims, "OH, MY GOD! I KNOW WHERE MY COUSIN LIVES!!"

"What do you mean?" asks Stephie.

"Dave's last name is Jones, right?" Tom nods his head. "I just read it on his license. And my cousin lives on Great Jones. I totally forgot. She told me she lived on Great Jones and that Great Jones was really East Third but not Third, it's kind of weird. But I forgot the Jones part, I just remembered her saying 'really East Third.' So that's all I wrote down. But that number must be the number on Great Jones and all we have to do is find Great Jones and we'll be there!!!"

"Are you sure?" asks Stephie.

"Totally," says Val.

"We're saved!" says Stephie. "We're saved!" Even though she hasn't been raped or killed, it has been a rough night for a sixteen-year-old from Ronkonkoma.

With a clear goal in hand—Monica's party on Great Jones Street—the threesome mobilizes efficiently. Tom jogs down to Houston Street and gets a cab. They pile Dave in and they get him back to his squatter's apartment, Tom carrying him up a flight of stairs. Then Tom comes back down and the three of them go off to Monica's. It's 11:45 P.M.; if they're lucky they'll be there in time to ring in the New Year.

42

Kevin and Lucy are making out in the bathroom stall of the Kiev. Then Lucy opens her eyes. Kevin's still really into it and his eyes are closed. Opening one's eyes while making out or making love is often a dangerous thing. It tends to be alienating. "What am I doing?" one wonders.

So Lucy eyeballs Kevin. She eyeballs her surroundings. The metal walls of a toilet stall. She pulls away from her friend.

"What's wrong?" asks Kevin. "What's the matter?"

"I don't know. I opened my eyes and I saw your face and I was like, 'Oh, my God, it's Kevin,' and I realized I can't do this."

"Let me get this straight. You saw my face and you realized you couldn't have sex with me? Is my face that bad or something?"

"It's not your *face*. It's not you, but it's kind of you. If we have sex, I'm going to be too depressed. We'll laugh it off—our New-Year's-Eve-Kevin's-Birthday Fuck—but it will make me sad. I know this whole thing was my idea, but I realize I can't go on forever having sex when it doesn't lead to anything."

"And you just realized this? You just realized this now?"

"Yes, I just realized it now." Lucy is upset, and she takes her winter coat off the peg on the bathroom door and goes out. Kevin grabs his coat, draped over the stall partition, and follows her into the Kiev.

She's walking out as quickly as she can and he catches up to her near the exit, by the cash register. He holds on to her arm and he's got blue balls, so he feels frustrated and a little crazed, and he says with a raised, angry voice, "So all the years of empty, meaningless sex with countless strangers and *bartenders—that* was fine! That was great! But this—with me, in the bathroom—one look and suddenly, bam! You have this epiphany where you realize you can't do it anymore?"

"Don't yell at me, please." Her eyes well up.

"You're crazy, you know that?" asks Kevin.

"I'm crazy? What about you? What do you call someone who just throws himself into one doomed relationship after the next when he could be . . ."

"When he could be what?"

"When you could be with someone who likes you, you know? Even though you're a failure, even though you have no money and no career . . . and even when you're being an asshole, like tonight."

Lucy begins to cry. A waitress bringing a check to the cashier hands Lucy a napkin.

"Thank you," Lucy says.

Kevin looks at her. "I'm sorry," he says.

Lucy waves off his apology, and opens the door to leave. "Where are you going?" he asks.

"To the party," she says and she leaves. Kevin goes to follow her, but then he stops. He sees that posted in the window of the Kiev is another flyer for Ellie's show. He hadn't noticed it before. There she is, wielding her ax on good old Freud's head. Freud, who tried to make sense of sex and love and dreams and despair. And Kevin stands there by the window and thinks about his relationship with Ellie. He knows where his heart belongs.

43

Hillary and Eric drag Monica across her loft and into her bedroom. The doorbell rings several times as they make this trek. They've already let in five people since Monica first passed out. Everyone is showing up at the last minute to bring in the New Year.

They hoist Monica onto her bed. She seems to be sleeping contentedly. Above her, on the wall, is the poster of her idol, Elvis Costello. The doorbell rings insistently. Hillary goes to answer the door. Eric looks at Monica with tenderness. *Poor Monica, her party is a success and she doesn't even know it.*

• • •

Val and Stephie and Tom pour out of a cab on Great Jones Street at 11:50. Val and Stephie are smiling. Tom is a little less happy. He still likes Val, but she isn't interested in him. He carries the package for Tony, careful not to lose it. The front door to Monica's building is open and they climb the four flights of stairs to her apartment.

• • •

Cindy gets out of a cab. Feeling empowered after telling Jack off, she has decided not to go home but to come to the party. She's a new woman. She walks into the building; she smells of dog shit, but she doesn't care.

• • •

Jack walks up to Monica's building. He's too much of a ladies' man to pack it in on New Year's Eve. Maybe tonight he'll find a girl whom he can sleep with, but who won't fall in love with him.

• • •

Kevin and Ellie arrive, purely by coincidence, at Monica's building at the same time. They hug one another and talk a little. Lucy, who had stopped to pick up cigarettes, sees them hugging from the corner. She watches them go in the building. She lights up and starts walking in the opposite direction. Then she turns around. *Fuck it.* She goes into the party.

• • •

Bridget gets out of the cab, which is still blaring disco music. Caitlyn pays the cabbie and gives him her matchbook. "Don't open it until later," she says. He drives off. She catches up to Bridget, and they enter the building together.

"For friendship," Caitlyn says, as they climb the stairs to Monica's loft.

"Yeah," says Bridget with less enthusiasm. "For friendship."

• • •

Miraculously, they all arrive before midnight—Kevin, Lucy, Ellie, Val, Stephie, Tom, Jack, Cindy, Bridget, and Caitlyn. They have survived their travails and have made it to a party. You have to be at a party on New Year's. You have to be.

So they join Eric and Hillary, as well as dozens and dozens of other people from all over the city. And when the clock strikes twelve, they all kiss and hug one another! It's 1982! A new year! The second year of Reagan! The 1980s!

And with the new year, the party really takes off. People are dancing. Drinking. Making out. There's smoke, rock and roll, and sex in the air! It's the best New Year's Eve party that many have ever been to. The food is destroyed and enjoyed. Somebody christens the toilet with the first vomit of the year. But who cares? This is the night for it. Bacchanal! Orgy!

Monica lies passed out on her bed, surrounded quite nicely by all the fluffy, warm winter coats of her guests. She dreams a dreamless sleep.

People keep arriving all night long. QB decides to come and shows up at one o'clock. Hillary lets him in. She's become the de facto hostess, and enjoys her role—it's probably the most rocking New Year's Eve party in all of downtown. QB gets a drink and sees Bridget, Caitlyn, and Lucy—all the girls who ditched him. But he doesn't care. All cares are temporarily lifted during these first hours of 1982. The music and laughter are too loud, the smoke too thick, for anyone to be able to really think about anything or care about anything. Even Stephie, in the middle of the room, is dancing happily, shaking her virginal hips to the beat of a David Bowie song. All is well. Happy New Year! Happy Fucking New Year!

44

It's January 1, 10:30 A.M. The sun sneaks through Monica's window and begins to peck at her face with kisses of light. She tries to open her eyes. It's like prying off a Band-Aid that she's been too scared to remove. Her eyes simply won't open. They're crusted shut. But, summoning strength, she forces her lids to rise up and reveal the world. They obey her command and she's disoriented. She looks down at her body. She's still in her dress. Where are Eric and Hillary? Then she realizes that it's sunlight coming through the window. She realizes that it's January 1. She sits up. Her head feels bruised, water-logged. The taste in her mouth is putrid. She has a grade-A hangover.

"Oh, God," she says, feeling nauseated. She stands up unsteadily and steps into the loft. Her home is destroyed. The floor is covered in cigarette butts, beer cans, paper plates, and the streamers that had been on the wall. And the balloons that had been on the ceiling are now also on the floor, like silver-colored fish that have died. The place stinks of stale smoke and booze. The odor makes her want to puke. Then Monica realizes that there is a live human being in the room. Stephie, fully dressed, is sleeping on the couch, with her mouth open quite unattractively.

Monica staggers over to Stephie and pokes her in the shoulder. "Hey, you, wake up," she says.

Stephie opens her eyes. She expects to see her mom. For a moment she thinks she's in Ronkonkoma. Then she realizes she's not. "Who the fuck are you?" she asks Monica. It's not too early for Stephie to start saying "fuck."

"I live here. Who the fuck are you?"

Stephie sits up. "Oh, you're Monica . . . I'm Stephie. I'm a friend of your cousin Val's."

"My cousin Val? From Ronkonkoma?"

Stephie yawns. "Yeah. She brought me here last night. What a night. God, I'm really hungover."

"My cousin Val from Ronkonkoma was here last night?"

Stephie looks at Monica. *What's with this girl, is she thick?* "Yeah, Val was here, and about a million other people."

"This is ridiculous," says Monica. "Everybody came and I missed it. Nobody misses their own party. People aren't supposed to party if you're not there . . . I mean I was here but I wasn't here. I passed out."

"I was wondering why I never met you . . . Well, the party kind of lost steam around four, four-thirty. That's when the neighbors called the police to complain about the noise."

Monica sits down next to Stephie on the couch. "The neighbors called the police? It was that good?"

"Yeah, and then the band packed up and left. It kind of fizzled after that."

"There was a band? There were actual musicians here, playing at my party?"

"Yeah . . . listen, do you have some juice or something?"

"In a second . . . I'll even cook you breakfast. But you got to tell me about my party . . . Was the band any good?"

"Real good. Somehow they heard about the party, and they came over after playing across the street at this place, Heebie Jeebies."

"You mean CBGB's?"

"Yeah, CBGB's. It was Elvis Costello's band. They weren't supposed to be at that CBGB's but they stopped in there for a few songs, and then stopped in here. They were really good. But I would have preferred the Boss—you know, Bruce."

"Elvis Costello? Are you bullshitting me?" Monica figures that Stephie is playing a cruel joke, that she saw the poster in her room.

"No, it really was Elvis Costello. They were just like roaming the city, playing wherever they wanted. I might pick up his album now." Monica can see that Stephie is completely sincere.

"Oh, God, I really want to die," says Monica, and she buries her hungover face in her hands. "The love of my life was in my house singing. And I was passed out under his picture when I could have been awake under the real thing."

"Look, I'm going to get some juice out of the fridge, all right?"

Monica looks up and snaps, "No. You have to tell me everything about Elvis."

"All right . . . just relax. What can I tell you? He has these thick glasses . . . Oh, there's one thing—he was hungry and this Hillary chick gave him some crab dip, she fed it to him on a cracker, and he made up this song right in the moment about loving the crab dip and wanting the recipe."

"It's off the box . . . I could have told him that. We could have had a conversation . . . I can't believe this happened to me. I somehow missed the greatest night of my life . . . Hillary put the cracker in his mouth herself?"

"Yeah, it was kind of flirty, but I don't think he was into her . . . I'm getting that juice. I need something." Stephie gets up and heads for the kitchen. Monica doesn't stop her. She follows after her and says, "At least they showed up. That's something, right? That means I don't have to live the rest of my life thinking I have no friends and everybody hates me. That's something, right?"

"Yeah," says Stephie, and she opens the fridge. The inside of the fridge is an ugly sight, everything has been torn and ripped apart. She closes the fridge, hiding the sight from Monica. "I think I'll just have a glass of water and get going," she says. "I have to meet this guy Tony and give him a package."

"A package?" asks Monica.

"Yeah, it's a long story. I thought it was drugs, but it's just a carton of Cuban cigarettes. I thought Cuban cigars were supposed to be cool or something, but this guy is into the cigarettes. Supposedly he only smokes one a day and not on the weekends so they last him almost the whole year, since there are only like two hundred or something in a carton and he only gets a carton a year. Anyway, I got roped into making the delivery . . . it's a fucking long story."

Monica can barely follow this. Stephie takes a drink from the tap, then gets her coat and package out of Monica's bedroom. Monica says good-bye to her at the door, then suddenly remembers to ask, "Where's Val, by the way?"

"I don't know. She left with some guy . . . Well, take it easy. Maybe I'll see you next year if you throw another party."

"Sure," says Monica, "good-bye." She closes the door. She's hungover and overwhelmed. Her little cousin Val went off with a guy. This girl Stephie is delivering Cuban cigarettes. But more overwhelming is that her party was a huge success. The police came. She's obviously more popular than she realized.

She gets a cigarette and sits on her couch. She smokes and looks around her. *Elvis Costello came to my party and ate my crab dip. Maybe I'll have a Valentine's Day party. Everybody will come. And I can send an invite to Elvis's record company. Dear Elvis: You were at my party on New Year's Eve. I was passed out, but I'm the one who made the crab dip. Please come back and sing me the song about it. Please. Please. I beg you. I beg you. I'll make the crab dip again. Let me feed it to you this time. Love, Monica.*

45

It's 11:10 A.M. Jack is lying on his futon staring at his walls, which are a veritable shrine to his budding acting career. Taped and framed and thumbtacked to the walls are all his clippings from newspapers, his theatrical stills, playbills with his name, and his different head shots from the last few years.

He is naked under his comforter and he listens to the toilet flush. Then Val walks into his room with just a towel around her.

She gets into bed next to him. "This is so cool," she says. "Your own apartment in New York City. I can come over and we don't have to worry about parents or anything . . . But I did call my parents just now. I didn't want them to worry too much. I used your phone in the kitchen, is that okay? I told them about you, but I told 'em I slept on the sofa, so you won't get in trouble or anything."

A shiver runs through Jack. *Trouble? Is she jailbait?* "How old are you exactly? Because you looked a lot older last night—"

"Don't worry, I'm totally legal. I turned seventeen last week."

Jack rolls over and hides his face in his pillow. "Oh, God," he mumbles.

Val rubs his shoulders, then turns him over and gives him a big kiss. His arms go to reach around her, but then he stops himself. She finishes her kiss and lies back contented on her pillow. For her, things couldn't be better. She's with a total hunk who has his own apartment in New York City. And he's an actor! And he can buy beer whenever he wants.

So they lie side by side on their pillows. Jack stares at the ceiling, feeling like death itself. Val stares at Jack, feeling like life itself. She's oblivious to his despair; he's well aware of her joy.

"You know, there's a reason I don't mind lying to my parents," she says. Jack feels it coming, like a kamikaze dive-bomber. "Know what it is?" she asks.

"I think I have an idea," he says, resigned. There won't be any last-minute appeals from the governor. He's a dead man.

"Bet you don't," says young Val, and then she snuggles up to Jack and whispers in his ear: "I'm falling in love with you."

The switch is thrown. Jack is fried. He lies there stiff, *amor mortis* has already set in. Val puts her head on his chest and says, "This is going to be so cool because we can spend every weekend together. And in June you can come to my junior prom. My friends are gonna be so jealous! Nineteen eighty-two is going to be the coolest year ever."

46

It's 11:33 A.M. Caitlyn is in her white terrycloth robe. The robe is partially open, revealing Caitlyn's voluptuous bosom. Her wet hair is up in a blue towel, turban style. She's sitting at her desk, calling Bridget. She lights a cigarette. On the corner of the desk is one of Caitlyn's little sculptures. It's a Barbie doll in a bright pink prom dress hanging from a noose attached to a gallows, which is also bright pink.

Bridget answers the phone. She's been awakened. "Hello?" she says groggily.

"So are you really hungover?" asks Caitlyn.

"I think I'm still drunk."

"That's the worst," says Caitlyn, and she takes a hit of her cigarette.

"So what did you think of that party?" asks Bridget. She's

waking up a little now, and so she sits up and gets her cigarettes, which are next to her bed, and she lights up. Across from her, on the wall opposite the bed, is one of her photographic self-portraits. Her freckles look very red and she's in a bright pink prom dress lying in a spider web and dangling above her is a big fake stuffed spider, the kind you win at carnivals. Caitlyn claimed that Bridget stole the prom dress idea from her Barbie doll sculpture and Bridget claimed that Caitlyn stole the prom dress idea from her photograph. But this was several months ago.

"The party was all right," says Caitlyn. "Eric was certainly all over that snotty girl who was the hostess or something."

"Yeah, and his ex, who I was so worried about and who was throwing the party, didn't even show up," says Bridget.

"I know, that's weird. And can you believe that lawyer-bartender guy showed up after we ditched him? That guy's a nightmare."

"He's not so bad," says Bridget, and she looks at the handsome, sleeping body of QB next to her. *Thank God I'm not going to be jinxed, too bad for Caitlyn.* "I spoke to him. He was really nice about us ditching him. And overall, I do think it was an excellent party."

"I wouldn't say excellent. Fair to good," says Caitlyn. "And more fair than good—most of the guys were posers. I'm really glad we agreed to go home alone, otherwise we'd probably be stuck with two phonies."

Caitlyn looks over with affection and satisfaction to her bed, where the dreadlocked cabbie is sleeping. *Thank God I'm not going to be jinxed, too bad for Bridget.*

The two friends listen to each other smoke for a second, and then Caitlyn says, "You want to meet for breakfast?"

Bridget looks at the sleeping QB. "How about a really late brunch?"

"Okay," says Caitlyn. "I'll call you later." Then Caitlyn looks out the window, sees that it's starting to snow. For a second she feels excited, like a kid. "It's snowing," she says to Bridget.

"I hate snow," says Bridget. "I don't have any shoes for it."

"Me too," says Caitlyn.

"Talk to you later."

"Yeah, talk to you later."

The two friends hang up and put out their cigarettes. Bridget puts her arms around her New Year's Eve lover and goes back to sleep; Caitlyn crawls back into bed with her New Year's Eve lover and does the same.

47

Eric and Hillary are making love. Eric is on top. He is working away, giving it his all. His face is in her shoulder, his eyes are closed. He breathes heavily. He pumps, he plows. Hillary lies beneath him. She tries to adjust herself, to get a good angle, but the damn guy seems lost in his own world. She feels like she's being bounced on by a large, hairless dog. So she just sort of gives up, lies there, and stares at the ceiling. Then she stares at his paintings, which are piled up along the walls. In the daylight she can see what they are. *Holy shit, they're all vaginas. I thought they were flowers . . . Oh, God, I wish he'd just come already and get this over with.* Hillary sighs and Eric mistakes this for a moan of passion, and this sends him over the top and he has an orgasm.

Eric rolls off her, squeezes her hand. They are silent for about a minute. Hillary looks out his window. *It's snowing . . . I have my heels, they'll be wrecked. I wonder if it's rude if I leave right now; I could explain about the snow.*

Eric also sees the snow. It looks beautiful to him. Everything is beautiful to him. He has proved himself. He's not a bad lover. But still he's dying to check with her, to have female verification, especially after last night, but he knows that's the worst thing a guy can do. *I can't ask, by asking I'll be a bad lover. Even what you do after sex can affect your rating . . . but I have to ask . . . I have to know . . . No. I won't ask . . . I'll be strong . . . Have to have confidence in myself . . .*

"So?" Eric asks, immediately caving in, unable to be strong.

"What?" asks Hillary.

"You know, *this.* Was it . . . you know?"

It dawns on Hillary what he's after. *Oh, Jesus, this is a nightmare. It was okay last night when we just cuddled when we were too tired. We never should have done it.* "Oh, oh yeah," she says. "It was great." She gives him a quick kiss on the cheek and looks at her watch. "It's almost noon," she says, "I better get going."

She sits up and gathers her panties and bra off the floor, and starts getting dressed. Eric is surprised by this sudden leap out of bed, but she thought the sex was good, so everything is fine. He props himself up on his elbow. "So you want to get together later?" he asks.

"Oh . . . Well, sure. If I have time."

This doesn't sound right to Eric. He watches Hillary put on her black cocktail dress. "If you have time?"

"Well, you know, if I have time . . . you know—"

"I don't know," Eric says, almost shouting, and he sits up. It's happening again. He's getting blown off.

"Are you all right?" asks Hillary; she doesn't like his tone of voice.

"I don't know. You tell me," he snaps.

"What are you talking about?"

"I'm talking about sex! Because I thought what just happened was pretty great. At least good. And I thought you felt the same way. At least you said you did, but I guess you were lying."

"I don't understand . . . you're getting all freaked about nothing . . ."

"Nothing? Did Monica put you up to this? Did she tell you about my *emotional problem?* Did she tell you to try to help me or something? . . . But you're thinking I can't be helped, right? And now you're running out of here."

Hillary puts on her shoes and coat. *This guy is losing it.* "All Monica said was that you were a nice person, and she was obviously wrong!"

Hillary heads for the door. *I'm getting out of here.*

Eric wraps a sheet around himself and catches up to her at his triple-bolted door, a real impediment to Hillary's escape. "Shit," he says, "I'm sorry. Sorry."

She looks at him. She tries to undo one of the bolts, but she can't. He opens the bolt, and says, "I'm sorry I was shouting. Please. I apologize."

Hillary can see that he's sincere. She relaxes. "Okay," she says. "I accept your apology."

"You see, it's just that last night was a bad night for me. It's kind of complicated. But can you just tell me one thing? I need to know the truth. Was the sex any good at all?"

Hillary hesitates a moment. "The truth?" she asks.

"Yes."

"I'm sorry. It was bad."

"Right," Eric says, and he hangs his head and falls back against the wall like he's been struck. Then he summons a little strength and undoes the other two bolts so that Hillary can leave.

Hillary feels bad for the guy. "Listen," she says. "You're good-looking and technically you're not bad. But you do go one speed. Fast. You need to mix it up a little. It made me feel like you didn't care what was going on with me. Maybe you didn't mean to, but it was like you were just showing off or something."

"Yeah, okay," says Eric, not really listening. But then he asks, since he's already humiliated himself, "What about the size? Is that okay?"

"Fine. Above average, even."

Eric, despite himself, smiles. A man will always smile if his penis is complimented.

"Do you want some advice?" asks Hillary.

"Why not?" he says. "I don't have anything to lose."

"It's something I need to learn myself," she says. "I don't think I can have really good sex with someone unless I really know them, unless I'm crazy about them. Try having sex with someone you're willing to fall in love with. I know that's what I need to do."

Then Hillary opens the door. "Take it easy," she says.

"You too."

And she goes, closing the door behind her. Eric thinks about what she just said. He feels inspired. *Someone you're willing to fall in love with.*

Still wrapped in his sheet like Julius Caesar, he picks up the phone and makes a call.

"Hello, Monica," he says. "Did I wake you up? . . . Oh, yeah, the party was great. Everybody said you throw a great party . . . Yeah, I see the snow . . . Look, I was wondering if we could get together tonight. You know, maybe we could have dinner or something . . . Seven o'clock? Great . . . No, don't bother dressing up. I think we should order in . . . Okay, bye, and I just want you to know I'm really looking forward to seeing you."

Eric hangs up the phone and heads for the shower. He feels like a new man. He may have been voted Worst Lover of 1981, but he plans on relinquishing that title in '82.

48

Tom and Cindy are at the Kiev, which is open twenty-four hours. They've been there ever since the party ended. All they've been doing is talking and eating: They've had pierogis, kielbasa, scrambled eggs, and pancakes. Also, at one point, Tom went out and got them a *Times* and a *Post,* and, like a couple that's been together for years, they sat across from one another and read their papers. Tom, despite his job as a roadie, is trying to improve himself and he read the *Times,* while Cindy enjoyed the gossip pages of the *Post.*

And now, after paying their bill—Tom's treat—they head up Second Avenue, and it's snowing. Tom thinks about holding Cindy's hand, but he senses with this girl that he should go slow, be the complete gentleman. He had gone for the kiss too soon with Val and that had really backfired.

When they come to the corner of St. Marks Place and have to wait for the light, Tom says, "So can I call you later?"

Cindy smiles shyly. "You mean, later today?"

"Yeah. Unless you think that's too soon . . . I don't want to pressure you, be a jerk."

"You're not being a jerk. You're sweet."

"Really?"

"Very sweet . . . so call me later."

"Maybe we can go to a movie."

"That sounds good."

"I'm glad you want to see me again," says Tom, being forthright *and* romantic. "Because I really like you."

"You do?" asks Cindy.

"I know it seems fast to say that, but I don't think a person needs a lot of time to know something like that. I think when it happens, you just know it right away."

"Yeah, right away."

They smile at one another, then cross the street. Tom decides it's okay to try and hold her hand and Cindy lets him. Both of them feel quiet and shy and happy. They are holding hands and it's snowing.

Tom walks Cindy over to the number six train at Astor Place. The snow is coming down pretty hard now and at the top of the stairs to the subway they linger, still holding hands.

"So I'll call you in a few hours," says Tom.

"Okay," says Cindy. And then they both get real quiet. He stares at her sweet, clear face, her auburn hair. She takes in his great height, his rugged, handsome brow. They know it's time. Tom lowers his head slowly and his lips find hers. She hesitates, then puts her arm around his back and draws him in close. They have a good, long, wonderful kiss. The snow is falling all around them. Cindy feels small and perfect in his arms; Tom feels large and perfect in hers.

When they part Tom is amazed, and it's like he's taken a truth serum because he doesn't stop himself from saying to Cindy, "You're gonna think I'm crazy, but I kind of feel like I'm falling in love with you or something."

"Oh, I don't think you're crazy," she says and they kiss again. Then they hear the subway, so Cindy says, "Bye, see you tonight," and she runs down the stairs.

Tom watches her go down the stairs, and even this small temporary separation hurts a little—he's in love. Then he notices, just before she disappears through the turnstile, that there appears to be dog shit smeared on the back of her coat. He remembers smelling it earlier and he thought he had stepped in it. But his love isn't affected by seeing dog shit on her coat. He finds it odd, but endearing.

So he smiles to himself and begins to walk home in the snow and he can't wait to call her in a few hours.

49

Kevin is sitting up in his bed, smoking. He stares at the glowing orange end of his cigarette. The woman beside him is awake but hiding under the sheet, trying to fall back asleep.

"You know," he says, "I was reading about how people protect themselves from emotional involvement by relating to their cigarettes instead of each other . . . that's what struck me at that party last night, watching all these people with their cigarettes. What is everyone so afraid of? Why are people so scared of each other?"

Lucy pulls back the sheet and, turning to Kevin, says, "You mean like us?"

"What do you mean, like us?"

"Well, we were scared of each other."

"No we weren't. In our case, there really *was* too much smoke in the way, we couldn't see each other."

"I don't think it was the smoke. It was other people. I thought for sure last night you were going to hook back up with Ellie."

"I saw you dancing with that bartender."

"Turns out he's a law student. I don't go for lawyers."

"Well, I don't go for women who take an ax to Freud."

"Yeah, I'm sure Freud could explain why we smoke so much . . . so why don't you put that one out and kiss me."

Kevin doesn't put out the cigarette, but he gently caresses her pretty face with his free hand and then he kisses her. She wraps her legs around him and draws him down, and he's still holding his lit cigarette in the air. Their kiss grows passionate, but then Kevin breaks away, not wanting to set his bed on fire. He puts out his cigarette and says, "I think it's time to quit smoking. That's my New Year's resolution!"

Lucy, from her pillow, her hair fanned out around her, smiles a smile that says "Yeah, right," and so he then playfully pulls the sheet over both of them and pounces on her for daring to question his resolve and they wrap each other up in a tangle of arms and legs and mouths—a tangle of love. And the cigarette smolders a moment in the ashtray, and then dies out.